Fallen Brook

# Love Everlasting

# JENNILYNN WYER

I

# CONTENTS

# COPYRIGHT

capable of generating works in the same style, trope, or genre as the Work, is STRICTLY PROHIBITED.

Cover Design: Jennilynn Wyer

Photographer: Ren Saliba

Editor: Ellie Folden @ My Brother's Editor

Formatting: Jennilynn Wyer

## Connect with the Author

**Website:** https://www.jennilynnwyer.com

**Linktree:** https://linktr.ee/jennilynnwyer

**Email:** jennilynnwyerauthor@gmail.com

**Facebook:** https://www.facebook.com/JennilynnWyerAuthor

**Twitter:** https://www.twitter.com/JennilynnWyer

**Instagram:** https://www.instagram.com/jennilynnwyer

**TikTok:** https://www.tiktok.com/@jennilynnwyer

**Goodreads:** https://www.goodreads.com/author/show/20502667.Jennilynn_Wyer

**BookBub:** https://www.bookbub.com/authors/jennilynn-wyer

**Books2Read:** https://books2read.com/ap/nAAgBb/Jennilynn-Wyer

**Amazon Author Page:** https://www.amazon.com/author/jennilynnwyer

**Newsletter:** https://forms.gle/vYX64JHJVBX7iQvy8

**SUBSCRIBE TO MY NEWSLETTER** for news on upcoming releases, cover reveals, sneak peeks, author giveaways, and other fun stuff!

## JOIN THE J-CREW: A JENNILYNN WYER ROMANCE READER GROUP

Join link https://www.facebook.com/groups/jennilynnsjcrewreadergroup

# DEDICATION

Only good girls get book boyfriends.

**[book boyfriend]**
(noun)
A billionaire, mafia, vampire, motorcycle-riding, grumpy single-dad rock star cowboy who is also an ex-marine firefighter with 8-pack abs, knows how to cook, washes your hair, never has morning breath, and does that finger-twist thing that sends you straight to heaven.

# SYNOPSIS

*Mason*

Aria Whitlock said she loved me, but I choked on the words and couldn't say them back. Wanting to protect her from my past and my darkness, I walked away from the only woman who ever owned my heart.

For over a year, the ache of her absence consumed me until I had no other choice but to move back home to Dearborne, North Carolina, determined to reclaim the woman I foolishly left behind.

Get ready, Aria, because I will do anything to win you back—including moving in right next door.

*Love Everlasting* is a second chance, small town romance novella that includes:
*a possessive MMC who will do anything to win back to women he loves
*a strong and sassy FMC
*forced proximity
*next door neighbors
*sports (baseball)
*love-hate banter
*angst and steam
*HEA

**Reader's Note**: *Love Everlasting* is a steamy, second chance, small town romance novella (25K words) set in the world of Fallen Brook: The Montgomerys. Readers begged me for Mason's story after falling in love with him in *Wanderlost* (he was Bennett's best friend). Mason returned in *About That Night* (he was Douglass's BFF with benefits). Now, he gets his own HEA. You do not have to read either book to enjoy the novella unless you want more information on Mason's backstory.

*Previously published as a bonus novella, Second Chance Hearts, included in the Fallen Brook Series Box Set Books 4-6: The Montgomerys.*

# DEAR READER

Welcome to my world of Fallen Brook, my beloved small town romances where you will fall in love again and again and again. I hope you enjoy Mason's novella, *Love Everlasting.* Mason is a reader-favorite character from my Fallen Brook: The Montgomerys series of stand-alones. He first appeared in *Wanderlost* as one of Bennett's best friends, and because readers kept begging me to write him a story, I wrote him into *About That Night* as Douglass's BFF with benefits before deciding, "What the heck," and wrote him his own novella so he could get his own HEA.

*Love Everlasting* is a short novella, about 25K words long, but I tried to pack it with my usual emotional heartstring pulls as well as throw in those Easter eggs I love to include in every story I write. You do not have to read *Wanderlost* (award-winner) or *About That Night* to enjoy Mason's novella, but I promise you won't regret it if you do! (*Side note: Wanderlost is one of my multi-award-winning romance novels. It won the 2023 Contemporary Romance Writers Reader's Choice Award, and was a 2023 HOLT Medallion Award Finalist, a 2023 Contemporary Romance Writers Stiletto Finalist, and a 2023 Carolyn Reader's Choice Award Finalist.*)

Here's the lowdown on some things you'll come across in the novella that refer back to previous books.

**Characters mentioned:**

* Bennett McIntyre and Harper Collingswood McIntyre (main protagonists from *Wanderlost*)

* Carter, Christy, Sorcha, Michelle (supporting characters from *Wanderlost*)

* Jordan Hammond and Douglass Donnelly Hammond (main protagonists from *About That Night*)

* Fallon Montgomery (A huge fan favorite character from all the Fallen Brook books. The Montgomerys stand-alones are about each of his half siblings, and he appears in every single one.)

**Settings and other miscellaneous things mentioned:**

* Fallen Brook and Dearborne (my fictional towns set in my beautiful home state of North Carolina)

* Carolina University (fictional university that most of my characters attend)

* Woodspire (fictional town in Texas where Jordan and Douglass live in *About That Night*)

* Houston Lone Stars (fictional Major League Baseball team Bennett plays for)

* The Wishing Tree (a.k.a. The Wish Tree. First appeared in *All Our Next Times* and is a symbol that I weave into many of my stories.)

* the #NEVERFORGOTTEN mural (painted by Harper and appears in *Wanderlost*)

# PROLOGUE

*PAST*

*ARIA*

*"Three... two... one. Happy New Year!"*

Standing next to the Wishing Tree, shivers dance along my spine as the chilly wind perforates through the thin wool of my peacoat. I flip the collar up and adjust my scarf as the wind whips the tiny snow flurries around and around like dancing wood sprites.

"I'm so sorry, Aria."

I watch Mason's tall silhouette disappear into the crowd of people.

Fireworks boom overhead, illuminating the snowy night sky with a rainbow of colors that fall to earth in a waterfall of sparkles. The cacophonic din of exuberant, drunken cheers explodes around me. Passionate kisses abound, celebratory hugs are passed around, and resolutions are made with good intentions as people—some are students like me who came back early from holiday break or never left, while others are locals or tourists—gather in the central quad of Carolina University to welcome in the new year with excitement. Happy people with wide smiles fill my blurred vision, and I swipe at the icy snowflakes that dust my wet cheeks and melt into my tears.

I thought I'd be one of these people. Full of cheer and excited for a brand-new year to begin. I thought I'd be ringing in the new year with *him*. The man I loved. The first man I ever trusted enough to give my heart to. The man who promised he would protect my fragile heart and never break it.

But Mason McIntyre is a liar.

He didn't protect my heart. He obliterated it.

I look up at the Wishing Tree adorned with hundreds of paper stars. Its limbs are barren of leaves which make the dancing pieces of paper tied on with string that much more fantastical. Like something from a children's fairytale.

The Wishing Tree is an old oak tree that stands in the center of the main quad on campus. Several years ago, three students decorated the tree with string lights and hung silver paper stars from its branches in memorandum of a friend they'd lost, or so the story goes. Since then, it's become a tradition for students to hang paper stars along its many branches—stars they write their most desired wish on. Once the paper disintegrates, eaten away by rain and the elements, your wish is supposed to come true.

How many wishes had Mason and I hung on this tree? Dozens?

I saw Mason for the first time as I sat under the tree's shade reading a book. He gave me my first kiss under the lights of its branches. And standing next to the tree, he broke my heart just moments ago as the gentle snow started to fall while revelers counted down from ten to one.

My gloved hands fumble with the zipper of my small backpack purse. The steamy vapor of my breath in the freezing air occludes my vision even more than the damn tears that won't stop. When I finally get the zipper undone,

I rummage around the haphazard contents until I find a pen and a napkin that I completely forgot I had in there. It's from the restaurant Mason took me to for our first date. The irony will do nicely.

Using my thigh to perch the napkin on, I scribble out a wish, barely legible because of how badly my hands are shaking. I shouldn't have worn this dress on such a cold night, but I wanted to look pretty for him. I thought the dark red color complemented my jet-black hair and green eyes. Christmas colors. At least I had the foresight to wear leather low-heeled boots and not the strappy stilettos my best friend, Kama, suggested when I videoed her earlier in a panic about what to do with my hair.

Rising on tiptoe, I impale the napkin on a dormant terminal bud of a twig, stabbing it directly in the center of the heart I drew. How symbolic.

"What did you wish for?" a girl asks, her eyes glassy and her words slurred.

What did I wish for?

I wished I'd never laid eyes on Mason McIntyre.

# CHAPTER 1

*PRESENT DAY*

*MASON*

Dropping the heavy moving box onto the white-painted wood of the wide veranda, I lift my damp T-shirt and wipe the sheen of sweat from my brow.

A shrill whistle sounds from the front walkway. "Showing off the ab porn already. You'll give the little old lady next door a heart attack. She's already been creepy peeping with her binoculars from the window for the last hour."

I look over to my left and sure enough, Mrs. Taylor is standing in her living room bay window, staring, while her tabby cat, Buttons, perches on the windowsill and lazily licks itself. I wave, and she smiles a dentured smile before letting the curtains fall back into place.

"She's harmless," I tell Carter.

With a chin lift, he gestures at my other neighbor's house. The one with the cherry red door and black shutters. "Have you seen—"

I abruptly cut him off. "No. And drop it."

"Jesus, fine. Won't bring it up again." Carter rolls his eyes and joins me on the front porch, placing the box he's carrying on top of mine. "You sure did accumulate a lot of shit in only a year while living in Tampa."

"Kiss my ass. You're just allergic to manual labor."

The front screen door creaks open and slams shut.

"Boys. Language," Mama McIntyre scolds, handing us glasses filled to the brim with sweet iced tea. I drain mine in two seconds and set the glass on the top rail of the porch balustrade.

Carter smiles, his dark brown eyes crinkling. "Sorry, Mama Mac."

I swear she blushes. Carter has that effect on most women. Half Haitian, half Puerto Rican, and a hundred percent flirt, Carter could swoon the panties off any woman he met. And did. Until he met his match with Christy, his fiancée.

Carter and I have known each other since the sixth grade. He's been one of my best friends since the day I beat up Toby Durham for pushing Carter into a locker at school. I have a tendency to use my fists rather than my words. The school-appointed therapist said I had anger issues. No shit, lady. Growing up in foster care my entire life, being passed from one family to the next, would make anyone angry. Feeling unwanted and unloved. Always asking yourself, "What's so wrong with me that nobody wants me?"

Not all the families I lived with were bad. The elderly couple I stayed with in Asheville for a couple of years were really nice. But my one true saving grace was the McIntyres. My other best friend Bennett's family. Bennett is the third side of my and Carter's ride-or-die triangle of brotherhood. The three of us grew up together, played baseball together, even went to the same university and lived in the same dorm together. Every good memory in the shitstorm I call my life involves the two of them.

Other than the time I was in Asheville, I basically resided at the McIntyre's house. Had my own room too. Becca McIntyre loved me like her own. When I aged out of the system, I moved in permanently to their house. It was home. The McIntyres were my family. Always had been. From the time I was a teenager, the townsfolk in Dearborne called me Mason McIntyre. I never corrected them. The surname Yancy written on my birth certificate held no significance to me other than as a reminder of the mother who didn't want me, and the father who walked away before I was even born.

I've always considered Dearborne my home, just like I consider the McIntyres my family. When I was offered the coaching position a few months ago to head the baseball program at my high school alma mater, I eagerly accepted, then immediately made an offer on this two-bedroom bungalow when Mama Mac told me it was up for sale. It was a house I was familiar with since it was down the block from the McIntyre's. Bennett and I passed it a million times on bike rides, on our way to the park, or when we took the shortcut through Mr. Hanson's backyard to get to Carter's house.

"You need some potted flowers. A little pop of color. I'll pick some stuff up at the garden center later. You also need to go to the grocery store." Mama Mac takes a seat on the porch bench swing and fans herself with her hand.

The roof of the veranda shields us from the intensity of the punishing July sun, but not from the pervasive humidity that chokes the air. North Carolina in the summertime can be a sweltering cesspool of misery.

"You left enough pre-prepared meals in the fridge to last me a month," I remind her.

She huffs at me. "Essentials, Mason. Milk, bread, butter,

fresh produce."

"I can get that stuff at home," I tease. The woman lives to feed me.

Carter plops down next to her on the swing, his long legs extending out several feet.

"Whose house are we watching the game next Saturday?"

Bennett is the only one of us to go into the majors after college and currently plays for the Houston Lone Stars. Carter and I love baseball, but we never lived and breathed it like Bennett. I didn't want that transient life anyway. Professional baseball players live out of their suitcase for the majority of the year, and I'd been shuffled and moved around enough in my life to know that wasn't what I wanted for my future. I wanted to set down roots. Have a semblance of permanency. A foundation for a future I could build upon.

Picking up the topmost cardboard box, I reply, "We can do it here. I want to try out my new wide-screen and surround sound. I'll call Douglass and set up a Zoom watch party."

My best 'girl' friend, Douglass, lives in Woodspire, Texas with her husband, Jordan, and his sister, Harper. Harper is Bennett's wife; she's also a Dearborne native and went to school with the guys and me. It's true what they say about six degrees of separation.

When my phone vibrates in my back pocket, I toe the screened door open with my foot and walk inside the house, carefully depositing the box marked 'dishes' on the quartz countertop in the kitchen.

Digging my phone out, I click accept on the video call. Douglass's gorgeous, freckled face comes into view.

"Hey, baby girl."

"Tell me a joke."

I met Douglass through Harper while at CU. It was an instant friendship. An instant connection. Kindred spirits. We were both damaged. Both broken. Douglass was the calm to my chaos, and I was the light she needed to guide her out of the darkness. Over time, our friendship turned physical. A 'friends with benefits' kind of thing, even though I despise using that figure of speech. We were just two people seeking comfort in the person we trusted most not to hurt us. When I met Aria, Douglass and I switched back to being just good friends.

"Why are men like cars?"

"Why?" she asks, playing along.

"They pull out before they see if someone else is coming."

Her burst of laughter is music to my ears. "As you can clearly hear, my husband doesn't have that particular automotive problem."

"I'm taking that as a compliment," Jordan says in the background, trying to calm their screaming two-month-old.

I lean a blue-jeaned hip against the small counter island. "Rough night?"

She has purple smudges under her hazel eyes and her dark auburn hair is sticking up every which way, but she's smiling.

"Eh," she hedges. "At least it's summer break and I can take naps during the day."

Douglass is completing her undergraduate degree in cognitive neuroscience at Rice. A dream she thought she'd never get to have, but one her husband made sure she got.

"Is your house open for visitors?" she asks, taking baby Cassidy from Jordan.

As soon as Cassidy is in her mama's arms, she quiets

immediately and grabs a fistful of Douglass's hair.

"You've got to be kidding me," Jordan grumbles.

"She's a mama's girl, aren't you, precious?" Douglass coos to her daughter.

Cassidy replies by yanking the clump of Douglass's hair she has a hold on, hard.

Wincing, Douglass narrows her eyes at Cassidy, who happily squeals and bicycles her tiny, chubby legs.

"So, it's like that, is it?"

Going back to her question, I reply, "You don't even have to ask. When are you looking at?"

"In a few weeks. Is the first of August okay?"

I do a mental checklist of my schedule. I have a few required meetings, orientation, and some teacher in-house days before the official start of the academic year, but those aren't until the second week of the month.

"It's a go."

Douglass bounces Cassidy up and down on her thighs in celebration. "Did you hear that? We get to visit Unkie Mason."

Cassidy makes a flurry of excited baby babble, her arms flapping like duck wings—then recreates the pea soup scene from *The Exorcist* and spits up all over Douglass.

Douglass drops her head back on her neck and beseeches the ceiling. "*Why?*"

"Holy shit, that was a big one." Jordan snickers.

I join him. "Now you see why I nicknamed her Little Monster."

Douglass glares at me, then at Jordan. She passes a very happy and wiggly Cassidy to her husband.

"Our daughter is part demon, and she gets it from your side of the family," she complains while looking down at her soiled T-shirt. Hopping up from the couch, she tells me, "We're walking and talking, babe. I need out of this nastiness."

I've stayed at Jordan's family estate while visiting Douglass and Harper. The place is massive. I notice a few of Harper's paintings hanging on the walls in brief blurs of color as Douglass walks out of the living room and heads toward the east wing where her and Jordan's bedroom is located.

"Anyway, like I was saying, we'll be coming to North Carolina first of August and will spend a few days at the Montgomery place, then head your way. Fallon is flying back from New Zealand and wants to meet his niece."

Fallon is one of Jordan's brothers. There are eight siblings in all. Three sisters and five brothers, all with different mothers. Their bio dad, Phillip Montgomery, was a bit of a cheating manwhore. He was also a billionaire. When he passed away and Fallon found out about the siblings he never knew existed, he took over his father's business, then divided everything up equally between the eight of them. Because of my friendships with Douglass and Harper, I was automatically welcomed into the Montgomery clan, and they became my family as well. For a guy who started out life with no parents, no family, and no one to love him, it's a bit surreal to have so much of it now. As Jordan's older brother Trevor likes to say, *"Sometimes the best families are the ones you create, not the ones you're born into."*

"Come whenever. You know you're always welcome. I've missed you, Dee."

I hadn't seen her in a couple of months, not since Cassidy's birth.

"I've missed you too." She nibbles on her bottom lip for a second, then says, "I also had an ulterior motive for calling today."

Holding the phone in one hand, I open the refrigerator with the other and scan the inside for something to eat. I spot a tub of cold pasta salad. Drawers open and close as I try to find a fork before I remember they're packed with the dishes in the box on the counter. I can eat with my fingers.

"And what's that?" I ask, but I already know what she's going to say.

My reason for coming back to Dearborne wasn't only for the coaching job.

Movement next door catches my attention through the kitchen window located over the double sink. My eyes track the raven-haired woman as she walks into her kitchen, fills the coffee depository with water, pops in a single pod, and sets it to brew.

Aria Whitlock.

I came back for *her*.

# CHAPTER 2

## *ARIA*

The hairs on the back of my neck raise.

But instead of it feeling like an ominous premonition, the tingles dancing across my skin feel electrified, like the static build-up in the air you sense during a thunderstorm right before a lightning strike.

The Keurig sputters out the last drop of coffee just as Brandon shuffles into the kitchen, sleep-mussed and barely half-awake.

"Morning, sunshine," I greet, and he grunts. I hand him the freshly brewed coffee I just made. "You look like you need this more than I do."

He must have no nerve endings in his mouth because he guzzles the scalding liquid like water. I reach inside the overhead cabinet to get another mug, then replace the used pod with the last one in the carousel. My nose scrunches up when I see it's hazelnut flavored and not breakfast blend. I add stopping at the grocery store on my long list of to-dos for the day.

Turning on the broiler for the oven, I grab the bag of bagels and take out two, halving them, then place the four rounds on a sheet of aluminum foil to toast.

"What's on your agenda for today?" I ask my stepbrother.

Brandon rakes a hand through his mop of wavy brown hair and shrugs. "Maybe hang out with Tyler, hit the batting cages, or go back to bed. I dunno."

Brandon Abernathy. Teenage apathy at its best. Then again, summers for seventeen-year-olds who are about to start their senior year of high school are supposed to be filled with nothing but sleep-ins and hanging out with friends. Enjoying the last vestiges of childhood freedom before adulthood comes knocking on your door. Besides, it's also Saturday, and weekends are meant to be lazy.

Putting his empty mug down, Brandon stretches his arms overhead and yawns widely. "Dad texted."

Mom and Dirk, my stepfather, are going through a nasty divorce, so when Brandon asked me if he could come stay with me for a while, of course I said yes. Brandon and I have always been close, and once the fighting between our parents ramped up last year and the divorce got ugly, I moved to Dearborne to be closer to him. And now, he's living with me full-time instead of with his mother in Idaho. It's a messy situation all around.

I never liked my stepdad, Dirk, and to this day, I still don't understand why Mom married him. The man is a grade-A asshole. Thank goodness, Brandon neither got his father's looks nor his father's pompous personality.

Buttering the bagels, I arch an eyebrow in question. The only time Dirk ever contacts his son these days is so he can dish out heavy doses of emotional manipulation. Mom, on the other hand, completely ignores me. But I'm used to that.

"Anything you want to talk about?"

"Nothing important. Just the same old bullshit."

I don't push. Brandon knows he can talk to me about anything, and I know he will when he's ready.

Setting the bagels under the broiler, I wash a few strawberries and cut them into thin circles. More awake after getting his caffeine fix, Brandon goes to the fridge and takes out the tub of cream cheese.

"Did you see we're getting new neighbors?" he asks, using the oven mitt to take out the slightly burned bagels from the oven. "The noise is what woke me."

I look over my shoulder through the kitchen window and see movement through the adjacent window in the house next door.

"Huh. Didn't notice."

I seem not to notice a lot of things. That's what happens when you dissociate from the world after having your heart ripped out of your chest over and over. First it was by a father who walked away when I was eight, then by a mother who pretended I didn't exist anymore because I reminded her too much of the husband who left her. Then there was Lucas, my best friend since childhood who turned into my cheating ex in high school. And lastly by the man I fell head over heart in love with. As soon as I said those three little words, he politely apologized and walked away. Just like my father.

And who does that anyway? What appropriate response to someone telling you, "*I love you,*" is to reply, "*I'm sorry?*"

Not wanting to think about *him* or Dirk or Mom, I hip-bump Brandon out of the way and take over spreading the cream cheese onto the bagels, then add slices of strawberry on top of each.

"Would you mind mowing the grass today?" I ask as we take our plates to the two-person breakfast table I have set up in the corner of the kitchen.

My tiny one-story Craftsman is small, about twelve-hundred square feet and only two bedrooms, but it's mine.

Grandma Whitlock left it to me in her will when she passed two years ago. There's no mortgage to worry about, only upkeep. Mom wanted me to sell it, but I refused. The few really good memories I have in my life are the times I spent with my grandmother in this house.

Brandon takes a huge bite out of his bagel, practically inhaling half. "There's a party tonight at John's house."

With his mouth full, I can barely understand what he's saying except for party and John. Internally, I sigh loudly because party plus his friend John equal nothing but trouble. Externally, I give Brandon *the look*; the one a mistrusting parent might give their child. In return, Brandon sends me a bright, innocent smile.

I like his friend John as much as I like my stepfather, Dirk. But I'm not Brandon's parent. He's also almost eighteen years old and needs the freedom to make his own decisions and his own mistakes. I could play the part of strict parent and tell him what to do or who to be friends with, but that's not the sister I want to be for him.

Licking cream cheese off my fingertips, I use those fingers to count off my demands one by one. "No drinking. No sex. No drugs."

His chair legs scrape across the linoleum floor when he sits back. "What? Come on, Ari! You can't take sex out. Janna is going to be there. That girl's mouth is better than a Hoover—"

"Stop!" Choking on the bite of food I just took when it gets sucked down my windpipe, I throw the uneaten half of my bagel at his head. "Jesus, Brandon, I don't need to hear that. There is such a thing as TMI. And show some respect. Would you want a guy talking about me like that?"

Wiping off the smear of white from his cheek, he scowls, brown eyes squinted and murderous, letting me know I made my point.

"I'm going back to bed." He gets up from the table and puts his dish with my bagel projectile next to the sink.

"Love you!" I cheerily call out when he grumps out of the kitchen.

"Love you too, even if you are a cockblock," he grumbles.

Do people still say that?

Taking the rest of my coffee with me, I push the sliding glass door open and pad barefoot out onto the small patio deck. Muggy air scented with honeysuckle envelops me as I rest my elbows on the deck railing, cradling the mug between my palms. The temperatures aren't as sweltering yet under the direct rays of the sun rising in the cloudless sky, but it's getting there. Wearing only a tank top and frayed shorts, pearls of sweat begin to bead down my back and along my hairline where my ponytail brushes against my neck.

I take a moment to enjoy watching the bees and butterflies flit around the wildflowers I planted along the fence line. The square plot reserved for the vegetable garden Grandma started a decade ago is in need of de-weeding. How many hours would she and I spend tending to the tomato and squash plants or plucking pole beans off the vine?

A faint breeze that does nothing to cool things down gently rustles the green, waxy leaves of the Southern red oak tree that sits along the property line between my house and the new neighbor's. Every time I look at that tree now, I'm reminded of the Wishing Tree. And of Mason.

It's been well over a year since he walked away and stomped all over my heart in the process, and like a pathetic, lovesick fool, I'm still pining over the man. I've tried to date. Went out a few times. My best friend, Kama, lives by the adage, "In order to get over someone, you need to get under someone new." Easier said than done. When you've had amazing, it's hard to accept ordinary.

That skittering awareness from before brushes a trail of shivers across my goose-fleshed skin. Cocking my head slightly, I look past the oak tree and glance over at the neighbor's house. My heart pitters a fast beat when a shadow moves away from the bay window that faces in my direction. For a second there, I thought... but no. My mind is playing tricks on me. That's what happens when you think about something too hard. The phantom thought becomes a psychosomatic manifestation.

*Stop thinking about him.*

I'll pick up something at the bakery tomorrow and drop by next door to say hello and introduce myself to the new neighbors.

"Shit."

My phone vibrates in my back shorts' pocket, making me jump and slosh coffee over the lip of the mug.

I wipe off one hand and retrieve my phone, unlocking the screen with my thumbprint.

**Kama: What time is your date?**

I groan.

My stepbrother, of all people, pushed me into going out with the assistant coach of his varsity baseball team. Michael would talk to me at every game of Brandon's I attended. Okay, he flirted more than talked, but I appreciated it, nevertheless. What woman wouldn't want a gorgeous guy paying attention to her?

Michael is nice. Tall, with a fit body and the prettiest brown eyes I've ever seen. Like melted caramel dipped in gold. He's twenty-eight years old and gainfully employed. Attributes a single woman would look for in a man, right?

God, I sound pathetic, even in my own mind.

After baseball season ended, then school let out, Michael and I stayed in touch. Texted a little. Nothing deep or soul-searching. Just the run-of-the-mill stuff casual acquaintances chat about. That dynamic changed when he showed up at my house last week, a bouquet of red roses in his hand, and asked me out on a date.

**Me: Eight.**

**Kama: Know where he's taking you? We need to decide on an outfit. The sluttier, the better. Wear that red spandex one.**

I frown at my phone. Is she for real?

**Me: That's a Halloween costume.**

The red dress she's referring to is the one I wore for Halloween our senior year at CU when I dressed up as a sexy devil. Mason looked mouth-watering in his... *stop thinking about him!*

**Kama: So?**

**Me: I am NOT sleeping with Michael on our first date. Hence, no need for slutty dresses.**

Three dots start bouncing as she types her reply. When it arrives, her message is a jumble of chili peppers, eggplants, peaches, and what looks like sideways spit emojis. Oh. That's just gross.

**Kama: Wear the dress! And remember to shave. EVERYWHERE.**

I send her a dancing middle finger GIF.

My phone rings.

"No," I answer, but Kama is already talking over me.

"You need some big dick action, or at least a few fingers need to come into play. Anything. I'll even accept heavy breathing in the ear. It's been almost two years, Aria."

"One year." One and a half, but I'm rounding it down to

one. I have my own way of doing math that doesn't make me feel like I'll turn into a lonely cat lady. "And it's still no."

"Aria," she whines, drawing out the 'a' sound at the end.

"Love you. Call you tomorrow," I say, hitting the red icon on the screen to hang up just as she screeches, "You better!"

My smile grows when my phone chimes a few seconds later with an incoming text message. Laughter bubbles out when I click the attached image of her holding a giant purple eggplant in one hand and giving me a thumbs up with the other. Where the heck did she get an eggplant? I miss her.

But she's right. It's time I give dating a chance. Move on with my life. I just don't know how yet.

Because the pieces of my tattered heart still belong to a man who didn't want them.

# CHAPTER 3

## *MASON*

Leaving the lights off, I open the back door to the house from the kitchen. The sticky night air hits me and humidity fills my lungs as soon as I step out onto the patio deck. Even after the sun goes down, you don't get much of a reprieve from the oppressiveness of summer. Then again, I'm used to it after living in Tampa along the eastern Gulf of Mexico for over a year. North Carolina doesn't even come close to the tropicality of Florida.

I lean back against the warmed wood of the house and look up at the inky sky. It's a new moon tonight, making the blanket of star-lit black overhead that much more prominent.

It's past eleven but I was too wired to sleep. The house was too quiet after Carter and Mama Mac left. My thoughts too jumbled.

Blowing out a weary breath, I slide my back down the side of the house until my ass hits the wood planks of the deck floor. With bent legs, arms draped over my knees, and hands clenched together, I close my eyes and focus on breathing. Inhale in for five beats, exhale out.

I don't like the dark. It's why I force myself to be in it. The only way to conquer your demons, your fears, is to face them. Stand up to them. Immerse yourself in them until the fear no longer controls you. The dark reminds me too much of *him*. Of being locked in that closet. The feeling of claustrophobia and not being able to breathe. My stomach cramping from hunger; my throat so dry from dehydration it felt like I had swallowed broken shards of glass. The pain of stiff muscles from sitting in a hunched position for long periods. And the smell. I still haven't been able to forget the smell of urine and feces that coated me like viscous tar because I wasn't allowed out of the closet to use the restroom. I only spent eight months with Troy and Pamela, a foster family I was sent to when I was twelve, but those eight months damaged me in a profound way. Mentally, physically, emotionally. I'm twenty-six years old and still afraid of the goddamn dark.

As sweat begins to build and the panic starts to rise, I squeeze my eyes shut and concentrate on loosening the constriction in my chest. *Just breathe.*

There's a swish of noise several feet away, then a feminine sigh.

Aria.

I know it's her without opening my eyes. If I was within a hundred feet of her, I would instantly know. Her presence always triggered a physical response. A visceral cognizance. Like having my veins pumped full of liquid electricity until every cell in my body felt like they would burst wide open.

The house next door is just a shadowy outline, but my eyes have adjusted enough for me to see her silhouette. The only times I saw her today were clandestine glimpses through the windows. I thought I had steeled myself for when I'd come face to face with her for the first time since that New Year's Eve. Clearly, I wasn't as prepared as I thought I would be. Having her so close now, only feet away, is like a physical punch to the gut.

Not wanting to give away my presence just yet, I remain quiet and watch, soaking up her nearness. Walking away from her was the hardest thing I've ever done. Gut-wrenchingly, painfully hard. And so incredibly stupid. I've regretted every second since.

I allowed those damn fears, my past trauma, to control me. Aria deserved better than me. I was too broken. Too messed up in the head. Too full of anger and resentment. Too afraid to let her love me and too afraid that my love for her would be pernicious and toxic. I didn't want my darkness touching her beautiful light.

It took me over a year, the love and support of my friends and the McIntyres, and one hell of a therapist to realize all the excuses I made for why Aria was better off without me were utter bullshit.

Aria's hushed voice floats in the air like wisps of smoke. "Why did you do that? Stupid, stupid," she quietly mutters to herself. "He just wanted to kiss you good night, and you freaked out."

She kicks the rail post of the deck, then curses and bends to grab her foot.

My chest feels like someone reached in and gripped my heart in a stranglehold. Some guy tried to kiss her? Tonight? If she was dating anyone, wouldn't Carter or Christy have told me? Dearborne is a small town that thrives on small-town gossip. If Aria was seeing someone, they should've heard about it.

She folds like an accordion to sit down on the deck, still muttering curses while briskly rubbing her foot. I can't take the thought of her hurting.

*You hurt her, jackass.*

As if she senses she's not alone, her head very

slowly swivels from side to side, carefully scanning her surroundings. Slowly, she turns and looks in my direction.

"*Jesus Chr—*"

Like a cat getting sprayed with the jet from a water hose, Aria startles and topples backward onto her elbows with a loud yelp that causes a nearby neighbor's dog to start barking.

With a hand clutching her heaving chest, she clambers back into an upright position and quietly apologizes. "I'm so sorry. I didn't know anyone else was out here."

At hearing her soft, husky voice after over a year, my heart jackhammers wildly and tries to punch itself out of my chest. I thought I was prepared for seeing her again. I'd practiced the words I would say over and over until I had them memorized and could recite them in my sleep. Funny how I can't remember not one of them now.

Not wanting to frighten her further, I keep my voice muffled and low. "No problem. I'm sorry I scared you."

I hear her small gasp at the sound of my voice, her head canting to the side with a flicker of recognition. I push my back against the wall of the house, hoping the pitch-black night keeps me disguised. Her green-eyed stare is unnerving as she tries to make out who I am.

"Do I know—" She abruptly cuts herself off with a shake of the head. "You must be the new neighbor," she says instead and thumbs over her shoulder at her house. "This is me."

I remain quiet. I have no clue what to say to her right now anyway. My tongue has turned to cement in my mouth.

Her hand drops to her lap. "Uh, yeah. Um... I'm Aria. If you noticed a guy pushing a lawnmower today, that's my brother, Brandon."

I'd never met Brandon, but Aria often spoke of him, so in a way, it feels like I already know him.

"We didn't want to bother you on moving day and were going to drop by tomorrow to say hi and introduce ourselves, but I guess I can do that now. So, hi. I'm Aria, but I already told you that." Even in the dark, her smile is blindingly beautiful.

*I miss you.*

Throat tight, I'm able to get out a lame, "Hi."

"Hi," she says again shyly, causing a warmth to spread through me.

Slowly pushing up with her arms to stand, she brushes off the backs of her form-fitting jeans. My gaze traces the outline of her curves as phantom memories of her writhing beneath me in bed overwhelm my senses. The sweet taste of her kisses. How her hair smelled like vanilla. The breathy way she would sigh my name when we made love. The sprinkle of freckles dotting her pale skin that I would connect with brushstrokes of my fingertip. How many countless hours would my hands and mouth spend exploring the wonderland that was Aria's naked body?

Aria fidgets, looks down at her feet, and exhales a gust of breath. With an embarrassed, self-deprecating chuckle, she says, "I guess you heard everything I said when I came outside."

"Pretty much," I reply truthfully.

I can tell she's nibbling on her bottom lip by the dip of her chin. It was a nervous tic of hers.

"So embarrassing," she mutters, then, "I promise I don't go around talking to myself. Okay, that's not entirely true. I tend to do it when I've got a lot on my mind and need an outlet for my thoughts… and I don't know why I'm telling a stranger this."

I can't stop the amused grin from forming. During the time we were together, she had a habit of mumbling her internal thoughts out loud and not realizing it. It was cute as hell.

"*There are no strangers here; Only friends you haven't met yet.*' William—"

There's a sharp inhalation of surprise. "Yeats. He's my favorite poet." Her head cants to the side again, and I can literally hear her brain processing things. "It's so weird."

She twists her long hair around her fist and drapes it over her left shoulder. The innocent sensuality of it has my jeans tightening uncomfortably behind my zipper. Aria was... still is the most beautiful woman I have ever laid eyes on. A mass of silky black hair framing a heart-shaped face and a pink Cupid's bow mouth. However, it was her eyes that I noticed first; the clover green so vibrant and clear from a distance, but up close you could see the gold streaks that swirled in her irises like a kaleidoscope.

"What is?"

"The truth to that quote. Can I tell you something that's going to sound a little crazy?"

My muscles vibrate with awareness of her as she leans over the railing and her warm sugar and vanilla fragrance hits my nose.

"Go for it."

"I can't explain it, but I feel like I know you somehow, like a sense of familiarity. Told you it would sound crazy."

My heart rate amps up several beats. Douglass told me something after she and Jordan reconnected and fell in love that has stuck with me. She said how true soulmates are meant to part ways, only so that they can find their way back to one another.

*I miss you. I love you. I'm so sorry for not telling you that.*

"That doesn't sound crazy at all."

She pushes her hair away from her face and climbs up onto the railing, dangling her long legs over the side and swinging them back and forth.

"Seeing as we've concluded that we're friends and all, can I confess something?"

I shift to face her more directly while still keeping to the shadows. "Go for it."

She tips her head back and gazes up at the night sky as if it holds the answer to her question. "Tonight was the first time I went out on a date in almost two years. Twenty months to be exact. That sounds even more pitiful when I say it aloud."

That invisible hand reaches back inside my chest and chokes my heart even stronger than before. Anger simmers at thoughts of her with another man. I know I have no claim to her anymore. I'm the one who walked away, regardless of my reasons. But dammit, that fractured, beating organ behind my ribcage still thinks that she's mine.

"I thought I was ready." Her voice is a sad whisper on the summer night's breeze. She lowers her face and looks directly at me. "You married?" She shakes her head in disbelief for a second time, her midnight pin-straight hair swishing over her shoulders. "That was really rude of me. Forget I asked."

Throat dry as the Sahara, I reply, "It's okay. And no, I'm not."

"Girlfriend?" Her hand smacks her forehead with a loud *slap*. "I am *so* sorry. I don't know what's come over me tonight. It's none of my business."

I assure her, "It's really okay. And there's no girlfriend either."

A beat of silence fills the distance between us. Only mere feet that feel like thousands of miles.

"Can I ask you another probably very inappropriate question?"

My grunted hum tells her to continue.

"Have you ever been in love?"

*With you. Only you. Always you.*

"Yes."

"Me too. I still am if I'm being completely honest," she replies, barely above a murmur. "It's why I couldn't let Michael kiss me tonight."

Michael.

Joy and jealousy, two dichotomous, dual emotions battle it out when I hear her say she couldn't let another man kiss her because she's still in love with someone else. With me. I know it's me. Just like I know I will never love another woman because I will always love her.

The heavy quietude surrounds us once more, but with her here, the darkness doesn't claw at me because she's my light.

Covering a yawn, Aria carefully hops down from her perch. "I think it's time I turn in. Thanks for listening to me. I'm sorry if I overstepped."

"You didn't."

She takes a step toward the house but stops. "If you're around tomorrow and not too busy unpacking, drop by for some coffee. I was going to stop by the bakery and pick up something to welcome you to the neighborhood, but I think I'll whip up some of my homemade chocolate chip cookies. I've been told they're the bomb. At least, that's what Brandon says... and I'm rambling again." She chuckles.

"Thanks. I may just do that. I'm a sucker for chocolate

chip cookies."

She used to bake them for me all the time. Hands down, the best I've ever tasted—other than her lips when I kissed her.

"Alright, well, good night." She turns to go inside her house but pivots back around. "I'm sorry, but I never got your name."

Now is not the time to reveal myself, so I give her my middle name.

"Andrew."

She licks her lips like she's enjoying the taste of hearing it.

"See you tomorrow for cookies and coffee. Good night, Andrew," she says, disappearing inside her house.

"Good night, ladybug," recklessly slips out of my mouth before I'm able to stop myself.

# CHAPTER 4

## *ARIA*

"Good night, ladybug."

I don't even make it a foot inside the house before my legs lock tight and my heart—the organ that hasn't functioned properly for over a year—comes back to life and slams against my ribcage so hard, I think it might literally burst right out of my chest and plop onto the floor beneath my feet.

"What did you just say?" I ask Andrew, knowing I couldn't have heard him correctly. Because there is no way in hell—no. It can't... no. Just no. Impossible.

When my eyes frantically seek the outline of where my new neighbor had been sitting in the dark, he's no longer there. For a second, I think perhaps my brain made up the whole thing. Him, our talk, how I felt both energized and comforted in his presence. The way my skin goose-fleshed at the warm, deep timbre of his voice. That sense of familiarity. How I felt like I'd known him somehow, even though we were strangers meeting for the first time.

No.

No.

*He quoted Yeats.*

*He called you ladybug.*

*The sound of his voice.*

*How easy it was to talk to him.*

*The damn tingles that shivered through your entire body from head to toe.*

Only one man has ever given me those tingles.

Mason *Andrew* McIntyre.

That son of a bitch.

Before I'm conscious of what I'm doing, my bare feet fly across the slick, dewed grass and run up his deck steps to his back door.

"Mason!"

My clenched fist pounds on the solid pressed wood, each strike filled with an intense rage that grows with every hit.

He knew it was me. He *knew.*

*How did he know?*

I thought I was opening up to a stranger. I don't do that for anyone. Not ever. I learned long ago that when you let people in, they just hurt you.

But I did for the stranger in the dark tonight. My new neighbor with the deep, soft voice that lulled me into a false security.

Did he think I wouldn't figure it out?

Right now, I don't really care because I can't see past the haze of red filming my vision. I'm too angry at being played for a fool to care about the fact that my ex is now my new next-door neighbor.

"Mason!"

A neighbor's dog erupts into a fit of wild barking as my shouts grow louder and my fist hammers faster. I'm probably going to wake up the entire neighborhood at this point.

The door suddenly swings open, and the momentum sends me stumbling forward and faceplanting directly into a very hard chest.

Oh, god. He even smells the same. A mix of sandalwood, jasmine, and bergamot. He still wears the Chanel Bleu I gave him. Without my consent, my nose presses into the soft fabric of his T-shirt before I can stop myself.

Strong, masculine hands grip my shoulders, and I automatically look up into a face that is still so devastatingly handsome, it steals the breath right out of my lungs. My eyes connect with navy blue ones that have haunted me for over a year, and it's like being punched in the stomach by a lightning bolt. His dark blond hair is longer, the tips curling around his ears now. His cheekbones look more defined, the short stubble of his jaw more alluring and begging for my fingertips to test its rough texture. The shape of his mouth is even more perfect.

Damn him for being more attractive than he was before. It's not fair.

His hands burn my skin like a brand as those dark blue eyes inspect me from head to toe.

"Are you okay? Are you hurt? What's going on?" he asks with concern.

The fist that was banging on the door automatically grips his shirt to hold myself upright on unsteady legs when his voice penetrates the fog of memories crashing through me. Memories that I've locked away behind a barbed-wire fence for the past year and a half.

The first time we met out on the quad. The way he would smile at me. Our first date. Tasting his lips for the first time. How he would tenderly stroke my hair as he read to me in bed. How being in his arms felt like home. Hanging paper stars filled with our wishes. The first time we made love. The night he walked away.

"How?" My question is whispered in the dark.

It's really him. How can that be? How can I feel both intense happiness and crippling devastation at the same time?

Our eyes remain locked, neither one of us able to look away. His face is so close, mere inches from mine, that I can see how his pupils expand until the blue of his irises disappears. His mouth timorously quirks up at the corners, the dimple on his left cheek becoming pronounced.

"It was the *ladybug* that gave me away," he says, almost like an apology.

A full-body tremor racks me when his nickname for me falls from his lips. Lips I'm staring at like a famished woman in the desert seeing a heavenly oasis for the first time.

"I don't understand. How is this possible?"

Mason's large, calloused hand tenderly cups my face, and my breath hitches, catching in my throat. That one small touch snaps something between us, like an overstretched rubber band that had been pulled taut past its limit.

I've missed his touch. I've missed his kisses, his face, his smiles, his voice. I've missed him so much.

In a blur of movement, I yank him to me at the same time he pushes me back against the open door. The windowpane rattles with the impact as our mouths clash desperately, our kiss brutal; one born of fire and desire and longing.

My body combusts into a ball of fire when his hands slide underneath me and lift me in his arms. My legs wrap around his lean waist while my fingers thread through his silky hair and grab tight. Mason deepens our kiss, and a needy moan of desire erupts up my throat.

"Aria," he says against my lips. Hearing my real name, not my nickname, is like a bucket of ice water being dumped over my head.

What am I doing?

I shouldn't be kissing him.

He left me. He broke my heart.

I detest this man.

*No, you don't.*

With a strength of will I didn't know I possessed, I push hard against his chest, breaking our kiss. Mason's harsh pants match my erratic breaths as we look at one another. The desire on his face makes my core throb, but I ignore the wants of my body and listen to the admonishments of my conscience.

*He hurt you. He doesn't love you. He couldn't say the words. He walked away.*

I hate how much I still want him, and I hate how easy it was for him to breach through the walls around my heart that I thought were impenetrable. Just one heated kiss has me almost forgetting the pain he put me through. The pain of losing him because he didn't love me.

"Mason, please put me down."

He does without protest, but he doesn't step away. His body heat scorches me like a wildfire, and I hate that too because I like it when I shouldn't.

Silence stretches between us, thick and uncomfortable.

"Aria, I—"

"No!" I reply more severely than I intend, not letting him finish.

I press my shaky palms to his chest and push again. It's like trying to move a mountain.

Panic tightens my chest, and my breathing becomes shallow, making it difficult to pull in oxygen. Mason must notice I'm about to lose it because he takes a step back. Then another.

"Please let me—"

I shake my head in denial. "I can't listen to whatever you have to say. I just can't."

I try to sidestep my way out the open door, but he lifts an arm to block me. And curse my traitorous eyes for lingering on the muscles of his biceps and forearms, remembering how much I enjoyed it when they used to cage me in as his gloriously naked body hovered over me in bed.

"Please let me pass," I quietly beg, needing to leave before I do something stupid like kiss him again.

It seems to take effort for him to lower his arm and let me go. As soon as I dash out onto his back patio, Mason's voice stops me in my tracks.

"I didn't mean for you to find out this way."

Giving him my back because I refuse to turn around and look at him, I ask, "Find out what exactly?"

"How I knew it was you. Why I'm here."

With quaking knees, I descend two steps but stop again when curiosity gets the better of me.

"And why is that?"

"I came for you, Aria."

Those five words slam into me with brute force. He came for me? He's known where I lived all this time but never tried to reach out or contact me until now? Why does knowing that hurt so much?

"Well, then, I feel badly for you because I want nothing to do with you. You're eighteen months too late."

With those parting words, I walk with a calm I don't feel back to my house. Of course, Mason has to get in the last word using a quote from Yeats.

"*'Hearts are not had as a gift, but hearts are earned.'* And I will earn your heart again, Aria," he says with a conviction that scares me, but also thrills me.

I glance over toward his shadow standing in his doorway

like a ghost in the night. Instead of Yeats, I reply with a quote from Javan.

*"Love can be magic. But magic can sometimes just be an illusion,"* I tell him, quietly slipping inside my house and shutting the door... then yelp when I notice Brandon leaning on the counter island, eating a bowl of cereal.

"Who were you talking to?" he inquires with his mouth full.

"Just mumbling to myself," I flat out lie.

I need to process what just happened. That Mason is here and living right next door, and not by coincidence either. I'm five seconds away from freaking the hell out and going into a total panic meltdown. Instead, I take out a bowl, spoon, and the gallon of milk from the fridge. Brandon slides the box of cereal my way. I'd rather have a giant bowl of cookies and cream ice cream with hot fudge and whipped topping, but malted puffs loaded with sugary marshmallows will have to do. I plan to eat myself into a sugar coma and pass out in bed after I take a quick shower. I guess my freak out will have to wait until tomorrow. I'm too emotionally exhausted to deal with anything other than feeding myself right now.

"How was the party?"

I'm surprised Brandon is here before midnight. He usually tries to push his curfew past one.

"It was okay," he replies but doesn't elaborate. "How was your date?"

"It was okay," I parrot.

His eyes narrow at me. "Then why are you upset?"

Sometimes I forget how perceptive he is.

"I'm not." I shovel a heaping mound of cereal into my mouth and avert my eyes, feigning interest in reading the nutritional label on the side of the rainbow-colored box.

Brandon places his empty bowl down on the counter with a loud *clank.* "I like Coach Michael, and I know I'm the one who pushed you into going out with him, but if he did anything inappropriate or made you uncomfortable, I'll kick his ass."

I smile at Brandon's brotherly protective instincts. "Perfect gentleman throughout the whole date," I promise him.

A perfect gentleman that I had absolutely no chemistry with. No spark or zing. Not like with—*no.* Not going there.

My casual reply only makes Brandon's brown eyes narrow even more before he says, "Uh-huh. I'm heading to bed."

I breathe an internal sigh of relief. Spanish Inquisition averted. For now. I know he'll bring it back up again. I need to learn how to school my facial features better. Mason used to say that I wore my feelings, and it made me too easy to read.

*Stop thinking about Mason!*

"Love you, little B."

"Love you too, big A."

I turn out the lights and head to my bedroom. When I go to close the curtains, I stop. Across the way is the window to the bedroom next door... and a shirtless Mason framed perfectly within its windowpane.

I shouldn't look. It's not right. I need to pull the drapes. Right now.

Unfortunately, my dormant libido woke up as soon as his lips touched mine and is now revving at the sight of his muscled, tanned back. He's broader than I remember. Bigger, more muscular. I stand frozen when he slowly turns around, like he can feel me watching, and my heart starts fluttering in my chest like a trapped bird frantically trying to escape its cage.

Mason reaches a hand out and presses it flat on the window glass, fingers outstretched as if he's trying to reach through it and touch me. His blue gaze bores into my soul, making me want things I know better than to want, because what I want is him. I shouldn't. God help me, I shouldn't.

I draw the curtains closed.

# CHAPTER 5

## *ARIA*

I pull my comforter up over my face with a surly whine when an evil spear of sunlight penetrates the crack between my curtains and hits me directly on my closed eyelids. When my phone chirps incessantly with incoming text messages, more than likely from Kama wanting deets about my date, I burrow my head under my pillow, hoping it will block out the noise. But it's the knocking on the front door that has me groaning out a curse. I slept like crap, if you call one hour of restless slumber after tossing and turning the entire night sleep.

When the knocking starts up again, I pull the covers back and shout, "Brandon! Get the door!"

It's probably one of his friends anyway. I haven't made any friends since moving here, so I know the early caller isn't for me. Is it early? I refuse to check the time on my bedside clock and roll over, hoping to escape the sunlight and fall back to sleep.

My bedroom door quietly cracks open, but inside my pounding head, it sounds like a firecracker going off between my ears.

"Hey, sis, there's a guy here."

"I don't know any guy. Go away," I grump.

"Is she seriously still in bed at ten in the morning?" a familiar voice says right before a heavy, solid body hops on top of me and yanks my covers away.

My gritty, burning eyeballs reluctantly open to see the happy, smiling, clean-shaven face of Mason peering down at me.

With sleepless exhaustion fogging my brain, causing me to think I'm still dreaming—because lord knows, thoughts of him are what kept me up all freaking night—all I can do is blink up at the man.

"What?"

"Get up, sleepyhead."

I yawn and try to roll over but can't. Dream Mason is annoying.

"Aria, who the hell is this guy? Do you know him?"

Brandon's question obliterates any lingering sleepiness, and I jolt fully awake. My wide, bloodshot eyes gape up at the man sitting on top of me. In my bed. Not a dream. Mason is really *here*.

I lie as stiff and unbending as an old plank of wood. Mason gives me a dimpled smile and a quick peck to the tip of my nose with a "Morning, sunshine," before sliding off me.

"I'm Mason McIntyre, your neighbor—" He points to one side of the room. "That way, and an old friend of Aria's from CU. You must be Brandon. Aria used to talk about you a lot. It's nice to finally meet you in person."

I remain struck dumb and speechless as I watch Brandon cross his arms over his chest and give Mason a thorough once-over like he's sizing him up.

"Old friend?" Brandon asks skeptically.

"Her ex. But I'm hoping to change that."

Mason turns and winks at me, and my mouth falls open

at his temerity. He did not just say that to my brother.

Brandon's eyebrows hike up, and his gaze pendulums from me, then back to Mason.

"Holy shit. You're *that* Mason?"

"Yep." The handsome bastard smiles.

"Cool."

*Wait, what?! Traitor!*

Mason joins Brandon at the doorway. "She still eat chocolate chip pancakes every Sunday?"

This cannot be happening. I woke up in some deranged *Upside Down.*

*Say something, damn it.*

"Mason."

Brandon looks at him quizzically, then at me again, before bumping fists with him like they're old friends. "Uh, yeah."

"Awesome. Lead the way to the kitchen."

I quickly sit up and cinch the covers to my chest when I remember I'm wearing nothing but a tank top and boy shorts.

*"Mason,"* I hiss through gritted teeth.

He looks over his shoulder at me, and a lock of hair falls over his forehead. How many times had I brushed that strand of hair off his face while we laid in bed, faces close as we shared the same pillow, and talked throughout the night about nothing and everything.

I shake the memory away.

"Ten minutes, ladybug."

"Mason—"

"Ten minutes or I'm coming back and will dress you myself."

"Don't you dare—"

The sexy, infuriating jackass grins at me and shuts the

bedroom door.

What just happened?

Grabbing my pillow, I shove it over my face to muffle my scream of frustration. I should have seen this coming. When Mason wants something, he's relentless. I should know. He even told me point-blank last night that he wanted me back. That he came here for me. Well, too damn bad.

Tell that to my stomach which is full of excited butterflies. Or my heart which is thumping wildly in anticipation of being pursued by Mason. Or the rest of my body which is now lit up like a freaking Christmas tree.

*Get a grip, Aria.*

Mason is the enemy. A gorgeous, mouth-watering, sexy enemy.

*He broke your heart,* the functioning part of my brain reminds me.

*Then perhaps he's the perfect man to put the pieces back together,* my heart replies.

Yep. I'm totally screwed. And not in the good way I'm now craving after last night's kiss. Stupid, perfidious hormones.

When my phone goes off again, I reach for it and ignore reading the half dozen text messages waiting for me and go straight to the source.

**Me: You busy?**

Kama's reply is instantaneous.

**Kama: I was about to call Brandon's number to make sure you were still alive.**

I hit the icon to call her.

"Are you doing the walk of shame right now?"

I throw my legs over the side of the bed and stand up. "No. And why are you whispering?"

"Then why haven't you texted me back?" she shouts.

Cradling the phone between my ear and shoulder, I yank clothes out of my chest of drawers. "Mason is here."

"Why are *you* whispering?" she asks, then, "What did you just say?"

I literally run into the bathroom, lock the door, and slump against it.

"Mason is in my house, fixing me chocolate chip pancakes."

Total silence.

"I thought his name was Michael. Geesh, what a sucky coincidence."

I place my phone on the vanity and hit speaker.

Shucking on the pair of sweats I grabbed, I reply in exasperation, "I did go out with Michael. But then Mason kissed me."

"Are you drunk?"

I pull the hoodie over my head. "Are you even listening to me?"

When I get a glimpse of myself in the mirror, I gasp in horror. It looks like I slept with a litter of baby racoons. My hair is a tangled, sticking-up mess, and I have black mascara circles under my eyes because I forgot to wash my face before collapsing into bed last night.

"It's kind of hard to keep up when you call your date by two different names."

I grab a washcloth, wet it under the faucet, add some soap, and scrub vigorously.

"Not two different names. Two different people. I went out on the date with Michael—"

"How did it go?" she talks over me.

"That's not the point."

"Then get to the bloody point!"

I rinse the washcloth and wipe my face clean. "You've been bingeing *Bridgerton* again, haven't you?"

"Aria, I swear to god."

"I went out with Michael. He was nice and cute and funny and..." But there were no tingles. None. Zilch. "When I got home, I went out on the back patio and there he was."

"Who?"

"Andrew. Ow, crap!" I yelp when my hairbrush gets caught in an impossible tangle. Screw it. I throw the unruly mass up into a wonky bun.

"Who the hell is Andrew?"

"That's what he said his name was at first. We started talking, and he was so nice. I felt I'd known him my whole life. Then he called me ladybug, and I knew. I *did* know him. It was Mason. Mason is *here*."

"Why would he say his name was Andrew? The only Mason I know... *noooooo*."

"Yes!" Finally, she's getting it. "Mason lives in the house next door."

"*Noooooo*."

I pick up the phone and unlock the bathroom door.

"Will you stop saying that? I'm freaking out here. He knew it was me. He said he came for me. That's just wrong on so many levels, right?"

"Well..."

"He looks so handsome, and he smelled even better, and I wanted to punch him in his gorgeous face, but I couldn't because we kind of attacked each other's lips. And the kiss. Sweet baby Jesus, the kiss—"

I touch my lips.

"Was it good?"

Dropping my hand, I scowl at the phone.

"Yes, it was good. Better than chocolate fudge cake, good.

And stop interrupting me. So, he said what he said. I was livid, then we kissed, and he quoted Yeats. Freaking *Yeats*, Kama!" I stress.

"I don't even know what that means."

"He used to read Yeats to me in bed," I try to explain, but she interrupts me once again.

"Skip over that. What happened next?"

"I ran away."

"You ran away?"

"Yes! But now he's here, in my kitchen, cooking me pancakes. Kama, what do I do?"

More silence. Then...

Kama's howl of laughter jumps out at me over the phone, and I'm tempted to hang up on her.

"You're not helping," I whine and plop down on the bed, tugging at a loose string on the bedspread until it unravels and snaps off.

"Babe, I'm sorry," she hiccups as she tries to simmer down her laughter. "This is fate or destiny or whatever the hell they call it these days knocking on your door."

My mouth purses to the side. "I don't follow."

The last vestiges of her giggles dry up, and Kama gets all serious. "You still love him, and don't you dare try and lie to me and say you don't."

I snap my mouth closed because that's exactly what I was about to say. "But..."

"But nothing. I know he hurt you. I also know that there are two sides to every story. And if you ever want to move on, you need closure. By some miracle of serendipity, he's there. You're there. Now's your chance to get some answers. No more what ifs and whys."

She has a point. I haven't been able to move on from him, no matter how hard I've tried. Mason was *the one*. My first love. My only love. And I do have questions. Maybe if I get them, I'll finally be able to get on with my life and stop existing in the past and the memory of him and what we used to have.

# CHAPTER 6

## *MASON*

I follow Brandon down the short hallway lined with framed family photographs and small watercolors into the modest-sized kitchen. Muted tones of slate blue and dove white cabinetry matched with cream quartzite countertops welcome me as I make a beeline for the stainless-steel refrigerator.

So far from what I've been able to see, Aria's home fits her personality. Warm and welcoming. It makes me eager to find out what she's been doing since graduating CU. Did she start her freelance editing business she always used to talk about? Whatever career she finally decided to pursue, she's clearly successful since she could afford to either purchase or lease this house.

"So, you're really *the* Mason McIntyre?" Brandon asks, getting out a flat griddle and large mixing bowl as I rummage the contents of the fridge looking for eggs, butter, and milk.

"In the flesh. Where's the flour?"

Brandon points to a row of four large glass containers under the left cabinet next to the sink. Each one has a label on it with Aria's precise cursive writing. I grab the one that says *All Purpose.*

"Vanilla extract and chocolate chips?" I ask next.

Aria always liked her pancakes sweetened with a hint of vanilla.

He walks into a small pantry and comes back out holding both.

"Thanks."

Brandon leans a hip against the stove and watches me get to work. I eyeball how much flour to tip into the mixing bowl. Mama Mac would cringe if she saw me not using a measuring cup.

"You're welcome. Now tell me why I shouldn't drop-kick your ass out of this house for breaking my sister's heart."

I look over at him and can't help the smile that forms. I know he's Aria's stepbrother, but right now, with his eyes narrowed on me and his arms crossed over his chest, he looks so much like Aria.

Cracking an egg open, I add it to the mixture in the bowl. "Trash can?"

Brandon toes open a bottom cabinet where a small trash bin is hidden. I toss the shell and wash my hands.

"How old are you?" I ask, adding vanilla and then milk.

"Almost eighteen. I'll be a senior at Dearborne High," he replies, handing me a metal whisk he gets from the drawer next to him.

With deft, quick strokes, I whip the batter.

"Then hopefully you're old enough to understand that people make mistakes. Ones they deeply regret making, and ones they would do anything to go back and fix."

He uncrosses his arms and opens the bag of chocolate chips. I pass him the bowl with the whisk propped inside. He dumps a ton of chips into the batter while I turn on the front gas hob to preheat the flat griddle.

"I do," he says in a way that tells me he has a deep regret

of his own.

I drop four pats of butter onto the griddle in a square pattern to slowly melt, then step out of the way so Brandon can pour four perfect circles of pancake batter.

When he finishes, I tell him, "I'm not going to make excuses for what I did, even though I thought what I was doing was the right thing at the time. I screwed up with Aria. Worst mistake I ever made. I just want a chance to make things right."

He puts the bowl down and grabs a spatula. "She's not going to make it easy on you."

A deep chuckle escapes. "I hope not."

I look down at my watch. It's been eight minutes. I was serious when I told Aria she had ten minutes to get dressed or else I would do it for her.

Brandon passes the spatula to me to flip the pancakes and gets out three plates from the dishwasher.

"You play baseball, right?"

A boyish smile creases his cheeks. "Yep. Centerfield."

I place the pancakes in a stack on one of the plates and pour more batter onto the griddle.

"I guess I'll be seeing a lot of you since I'm your new coach."

His eyes go round with surprise. "No shit?"

"No shit."

"Cool."

We both turn when there's a crash as a harried-looking Aria slides across the linoleum floor in socked feet and careens into a chair.

"Ten minutes exactly," I tell her, and she glowers at me.

"Not like I had a choice," she grumbles, righting herself and tugging her shirt back into place.

Her hair is a mess, she's wearing baggy sweatpants and

the ugliest argyle socks I've ever seen, and her face is scrubbed clean of makeup. I can see the smattering of freckles that bridge her nose. She has never looked more beautiful.

"Coffee?"

Her scowl could melt iron. "No, thank you."

Brandon supersedes. "On it."

Her frown transfers from me to her brother before landing back on me.

I innocently smile and hold the plate out to her. "Breakfast is ready."

She plants her hands on her hips like Mama Mac does when she's irritated with something Bennett or I have done.

"I remembered to add vanilla."

Her hands drop to her side.

"And melted butter."

With a huff, Aria snatches the plate and the fork I'm also holding and stomps over to the small eating table. When the single cup coffee maker spits out the last of the coffee, I add two yellow packets of sweetener I find in a dish next to the machine and walk the mug over to Aria. She's quietly sitting at the table, food untouched, watching me.

"I don't understand you," she says as I place the steaming coffee in front of her.

"Understand what?"

Her chin dips to her chest and she shakes her head slightly. "That you remembered I like vanilla extract in my pancake batter or the way I take my coffee."

Gripping the back of her chair, I lean over her shoulder until my lips are a breath's-width away from her ear. The late morning sun shines through the sliding glass door and illuminates the goose bumps that prickle up along her neck.

"I remember *everything*, ladybug."

She sucks in a deep inhalation and holds it, then slowly blows it out when I stand back up and walk around to the other side of the table and take a seat. Brandon brings two plates of food with him and sits down next to Aria, who's already shoveled a forkful of fluffy pancakes into her mouth. Her eyes close and she moans at the first bite, like it's the most delicious thing she's ever tasted. My jeans get a bit uncomfortable when my dick perks up at hearing her make that sound. *Not today buddy.*

"Did Mason tell you he's the new head baseball coach at school?" Brandon tells Aria as he slides me a plate across the table.

Her fork arrests in front of her mouth and her gorgeous green eyes meet mine. "No, he didn't," she replies with her mouth full. She swallows, takes a sip of coffee, and asks her brother, "Didn't you already have breakfast?"

Rolling a pancake like a burrito, he shoves the entire thing in his mouth. "Yeah," he muffles, rolling a second pancake just like he did the first one.

"Can you eat somewhere else then? I need to have a word with Mason. In private," she adds.

Brandon rolls his eyes in the same way Aria does, and I tamper the grin that twitches the corners of my mouth.

"Fine. I'm supposed to meet up with Danny at the batting cages anyway. Hey, would you mind if I picked your brain about something?" he asks me, standing up from the table.

"Sure."

"No," Aria says at the same time.

We both ignore her.

"I'm having trouble with follow through on my swing. I think it may be my grip, but I'm not sure."

"How about I drop by later today once we get back—"

Aria's fork clanks on the plate when she drops it. "We're not going anywhere together."

"—and you can hit some balls for me in the backyard so I can see your form."

His face alights. "Awesome. Thanks, man."

"Absolutely."

We bump fists.

"See you later." Brandon kisses the top of his sister's head.

As soon as he leaves, Aria whisper-hisses, "You will not use my brother to weasel your way back into my life again. He's been through enough with the divorce and doesn't need you pretending to be his friend."

I reach across the tabletop and take her hand. "Your mom and Dirk are getting a divorce?"

I knew she never liked her stepfather, but she loves Brandon like he's her flesh and blood.

She stares down at where our hands are connected, then carefully extricates hers and places it in her lap.

"That's why he's living with me. Things with his dad aren't that great right now."

The subject of parents is a touchy one for me for obvious reasons, seeing as mine abandoned me to live out my life being tossed around from foster family to foster family.

"First, I'm not pretending to be his friend, and I'm insulted that you'd think that lowly of me, regardless of what happened between us."

Her expression turns contrite.

"Second, if you ever want to talk, I'm here."

Her apologetic demeanor vanishes, and fiery green eyes flash a warning at me from across the table.

"For how long this time, Mason? How long will it take

before you walk away again?" she snaps, then thins her lips to stop from saying anything more.

I could promise her never again. I could spout off how I'm in love with her, have been from the beginning but was too scared to say the words. How I want a second chance. That I will do anything to get that chance. That she's it for me. My forever. The woman I see my future with. My wife. The mother to our children.

But I don't say any of those things because she wouldn't believe me if I tried. Actions speak louder than words.

"Finish eating. I want to take you somewhere."

"No."

"Yes."

"No, Mason."

# CHAPTER 7

*ARIA*

I stare out the window as we drive, watching the roadside scenery pass by in a blur. I say no, Mason says yes, and here we are, in his truck, driving to who knows where. I silently curse my stupid, weak, broken heart that is still in love with the jackass sitting in the driver's seat. I've been silently fuming for the past ten minutes, trying valiantly to slap mortar onto the cracks forming in the crumbling brick wall around my heart, but it's hard to do when he smells so good and looks so good and is so close that I can reach over and touch him and... I'm pathetic.

Eventually, I can't take the silence any longer.

"Where are you taking me?"

"You talking to me now?" he asks, glancing over in my direction as he slows down at a four-way stop before turning right.

I hold back my sassy retort and turn my head to glare at him. He returns my glare with a disarming, charming smile, just like he did earlier in the kitchen, and I literally melt into a puddle in my seat, which only irritates me more. Because, god help me, all I want to do is relive the kiss from last night. Feel his soft, full lips on mine again. On my skin. My body.

"Baby, you keep looking at me like that and I'm going to —"

I snap out of my lust-filled daydream. "I'm not looking at you like anything," I lie, and to give my pounding chest a chance to calm down, I attack the radio console, turning it on and hitting buttons until I find a decent song.

I sit back in my seat, the buttery, beige leather cushioning me like a pillow. "Is this new?" I ask.

I'm not used to driving shotgun in a huge crew cab the size of a small house. My car is a POS white Honda I bought used. It already had ninety thousand miles on it. I'm honestly surprised it hasn't fallen to pieces by now, but my little Accord is a tough old thing.

"How can you tell?"

"New car smell," I reply.

He nods once and hits the blinker to indicate a left turn. Even though I've lived in Dearborne for over a year, I haven't gone exploring much. Okay, I haven't gone exploring at all. It's really a beautiful town. Gorgeous area that packs an abundance of small-town charm. I love how everything is flush with greenery and trees, unmarred by construction and concrete.

"What are you doing these days?" he asks, and seeing as I opened the door for conversation, I reply, "What do you mean?"

"Job wise. Did you ever start your freelance business?"

Again, I'm caught off guard by the fact he remembers that, just like how he remembered I eat chocolate chip pancakes every Sunday or how I take my coffee.

Biting my bottom lip to stop the pride from showing, I nod. I was an English major, my head forever between the pages of a book. During my sophomore year, I helped a friend from class copy edit their novel and kind of fell in love with the process.

"You did? Aria, that's fantastic. Tell me."

Those denim blue eyes briefly turn my way, but I don't miss the happiness that shines in them or the way seeing that happiness makes me happy as well. Mason may have his faults, but when we were together, he was a fantastic boyfriend. Always supportive of my dumb ideas. Always attentive and listened to my silly ramblings with rapt attention, like what I said was the most interesting thing in the world. It's just the ending of us that sucks. It was so sudden and unexpected. And it hurt.

I look out the passenger side window. At the world flying by. It's a euphemism for my life this past year and a half. I've let it fly by. Time I won't be able to get back. Things I could have done but didn't. New experiences I could have had.

And it makes me wonder...

Like Kama said, maybe I'm looking at things the wrong way. Maybe seeing Mason again *isn't* such a bad thing. Maybe it's my opportunity to get some closure, find resolve with what happened, so I can finally move on with my life. Maybe we can end things the right way—as friends. It would be good if we could since he's living right next door to me. It would make things less awkward in the long run.

I shift in my seat to see him better.

"After graduating CU, I enrolled online at the University of Chicago and got my certification six months ago. While completing that, I created an LLC and was lucky enough to know a few authors I had met on Instagram that were willing to give me a chance. I copy edit, but I also proofread, beta read, and do developmental editing. My clientele is mostly romance authors... what?" I ask when his smile keeps growing as I ramble.

He parks the truck and turns the ignition off.

"Nothing."

My chin dips in incredulity at his non-answer, and I cross my arms over my chest, getting defensive as my cheeks grow warm with embarrassment for going on about my work like an idiot.

Mason reaches over the center console and brushes a hand down my cheek. My breath stills at the gentle contact, and I have to force my eyelids not to flutter close.

"Hey, don't do that."

"Do what?"

"Shut down. I love listening to you talk. I want to know everything."

"Then why were you smiling?"

It's a stupid question brought on by my own insecurities. For some insane reason, I want Mason to be proud of me for following my dream and accomplishing exactly what I said I wanted to do.

"Because I'm happy."

*Oh.* I wasn't expecting that answer.

"Because I've missed this. I've missed you," he continues.

I *definitely* wasn't expecting *that* answer. And if I were spouting self-truths, I've missed him too.

I turn the tables on him and ask, "Where did you go after graduation?"

"Tampa. Hated it."

Mason glides a finger down the curve of my neck; his touch is seductive, and it takes everything in me not to moan when his fingertips trace a line from my neck down my arm to my wrist.

He shouldn't touch me like this. I shouldn't let him. It'll only blur the lines I just mentally drew in the sand about us becoming friends.

But I don't stop him. Nor do I stop him when he leans

over and lightly kisses my temple near my ear, causing a million fluttery pinpricks of need to erupt all over my skin and cascade down my body like a sensual waterfall.

"We're here," he whispers in that husky, deep voice I remember so well and dream about often.

Not able to break free of the magic his simple, chaste kiss has me under, all I can do it utter, "Huh?"

The driver's side door shuts, breaking me from the spell, and I look around, trying to figure out where we are.

Mason opens my door and offers his hand to help me down.

"This is where you wanted to take me?" I ask in confusion when I see the letters spelling out "Dearborne High School" on the concrete and brick façade of the enormous building. "To Brandon's school?"

As soon as my feet touch the parking lot, Mason threads our fingers together and starts walking, not giving me an option but to follow.

I tug on my hand. "Mason, I don't—"

"I never told you about my past. About my childhood growing up or what happened here," he says, and it's the desolate tone of his voice that shuts me up. The pain I can hear that's infused in every spoken word.

I think back to all our conversations and realize he's right. Mason called his best friends, Bennett and Carter, his brothers, and I chalked it up to how close they were and assumed he said it because he was an only child. However, when I would ask about his parents, where he grew up, his childhood, or anything too personal, Mason would change the subject. Funny how I never picked up on that or thought it was odd. My vision was clouded by the rose-tinted glasses of falling in love, I guess.

I don't ask him what he meant by *what happened here.*

Because I already know, and it's not only from the news and newspaper reports I saw. Brandon goes here, so it's impossible not to know about the horrific school shooting that took place six years ago. My stomach curdles when understanding slams into me. Mason never told me the name of the town he was from, only that it was a small town in the Appalachian region of the state.

Under the low angle of the sun, the building casts a long shadow, and the remaining dew stubbornly clinging to the grass dampens my toes sticking out of my sandals. As Mason leads me around the back of the school, several sports fields come into view, including a baseball field and football field with a running track circling its perimeter. The aluminum bleachers reflect the sunlight with piercing accuracy, and I regret not bringing my sunglasses with me. At least the shade helps lessen the scorching rays of the late summer sun, even if it does nothing to tamp down the high humidity that suffocates the air. I'm already sweaty in too many uncomfortable places.

"We never talk about it for obvious reasons," Mason says, and I squeeze his hand that's holding mine. I can feel the slight tremor in his grip.

"Mason, you don't have to talk about it now. We can leave."

He shakes his head, a curled lock of his blond hair falling across his forehead. "I should have told you before, but I was scared. I never wanted the dark parts of my life to ever touch you. To change how you felt about me."

My feet stumble and trip over themselves, taken by surprise at his confession.

"Harper painted this," he says when we reach a large storage shed with the beautiful mural painted over its south-facing exterior wall.

Harper was his friend Bennett's fiancée at CU. They all grew up together: her, Mason, Bennett, Carter, Carter's girlfriend Christy, and another girl, Michelle. Douglass and Sorcha were the only ones from that group of friends who were newbies, like me. I can't tell you how many hours I spent with them hanging out, going to the beach, studying together. I envied how close they all were. The tight bonds of love they shared that went beyond just being friends. They were a family in every sense of the word. And now I know why. Tragedy has a way of forging unbreakable bonds.

Why would he think me knowing would change how I felt about him? I loved him. What happened here wasn't his fault. Like his friends and the other students, they were the victims. They are survivors.

I look up at the enormous painting. There are smiling faces of young people, *too many people*, I think, and tears spill over as I trace the mural with my eyes, soaking in every fine detail and brush stroke. A colorful set of handprints, each with a name and a year, create a border around the pictures, and in the middle, #NEVERFORGOTTEN is painted in bright, bold colors.

"I was a senior when it happened," Mason softly says, touching one of the faces.

I let go of his hand to wrap my arms around him. I need to hold him. To comfort him. To comfort myself because I could have lost him before I ever got a chance to meet him. I would never have felt the joy of falling in love for the first time. Never would have seen his smile or heard his beautiful laughter. The world would have been an emptier place without Mason McIntyre in it.

Not even my anger or my broken heart can compete with the immense gratitude I feel right then to have him here, with me.

"Thank you for showing me."

My arms tighten around his waist when he places a soft kiss on the top of my head, and I bury my tear-streaked face in his chest, breathing him in. Drowning in him. Never wanting to let him go.

As the hot breeze trickles around us, we stand in front of the memorial Harper painted, and I listen to Mason tell me about that day.

# CHAPTER 8

## *ARIA*

"Are you serious? How did we not know this?" Kama asks, then drops her phone so all I see is the ceiling of her living room. "Sorry."

My phone sits propped upright in its stand on the counter, allowing me to cook and talk at the same time.

"That's what I keep asking myself. Mason and I were together for a year, and I hung out with his friends on the regular. I feel so stupid. They all went through this huge, horrible thing. Something that would change a person in fundamental ways."

"What do you want to happen now?" she asks, lying back on her sofa, her rich, sable hair spreading out around her face like a halo.

Isn't that the one-million-dollar question?

Somehow, my need for closure turned into a desire for Mason and me to become friends, and now... now, I don't know what I want. My mind is a jumbled and confused mess when it comes to that man.

Holding the lid to the top of the pot at a slight angle, I drain the pasta in the sink, making sure to use oven mitts so the scorching steam doesn't burn my fingertips off. Brandon keeps threatening to gift me a colander for

Christmas. It would make it easier, I guess, but this was how my grandma did it and how she taught me to do it.

I place the pot down, set the lid aside, and add in pesto sauce, chopped garlic, and shaved parmesan.

To answer her question, I reply, "Now, I'm making dinner."

What I don't disclose to Kama is that I'm making one of Mason's favorite meals, pesto pasta, and plan to take it over to him along with the rotisserie chicken I went out and bought an hour ago. I'm justifying the meal as a house-warming slash welcome-to-the-neighborhood gift. Which is a total lie, of course.

"I think Brandon has a bro-crush on him."

"I think you do, too, without the bro part," Kama singsongs, and I aim a perfect glare at her grinning face.

Ignoring that, I continue. "Mason is the new baseball coach at Brandon's school."

She bursts out laughing. "Girl, you are so screwed."

I wave the long, wooden spoon at my phone. "Stop interrupting me. Anyway, after we got back, they spent two hours in the back yard together doing baseball stuff."

"Baseball stuff," she deadpans. "Got it."

I roll my eyes and scoop the pasta into a glass baking pan, then cover it with aluminum foil.

"You know I was never good with sports jargon." Propping my elbows on the countertop in front of my phone, I rest my chin in the palm of my hand. "I may have window-stalked them for a while. Watching them together and seeing how happy Brandon was—he hasn't smiled much lately. It was good to see, but it also made me sad. Dirk never did that kind of stuff with him. He never even showed up to any of Brandon's games. It was always Mom and me."

Kama bites her bottom lip and nods. "Brandon is going to be okay because he's lucky enough to have you. And you've got me. Sista friends to the end."

"I miss you, Kama Llama."

She playfully sticks out her tongue in mock disgust. "I think we can retire that little nickname."

I gasp. "Never."

"And I miss you too... Maria."

Standing, I snatch the phone to carry with me when the front doorbell rings. "Maria?"

"Aria plus Mason equals Maria."

"Yeah, that's a no," I tell her. "Hold on, babe, there's someone at the door."

"Hopefully a shirtless, bare-chested, dripping wet, right out of the shower Mason needing to borrow a cup of sugar."

"Muting you now," I tell her as I swing the door open to find not Mason, but Michael standing on my front porch. As in, last night's date, Michael.

Unmuting Kama, I utter, "I need to call you back."

"Wait! Was I right? Is it—"

I end the video call.

"Um, hi?" I ask, brows furrowed and confused as to why he's here.

Michael shoves his hands in the front pockets of his jeans and shuffles his feet in an adorably shy way. He looks over his shoulder, then back at me.

"Hi. I hope it's okay that I stopped by like this. I was in the neighborhood and wanted to say hi... so, hi."

His mouth spreads in a slow smile, and I can't help but return it.

Michael is a nice guy. Cute. Funny. Sweet. Has a well-paying job and coaches little league baseball during the summer, so likes kids. Left a huge tip for our waitress last night which is always a plus in my book. He's everything a woman like me should want—if it weren't for the man who unexpectedly popped back into my life and is currently living next door.

Wait a minute. I backtrack a few thoughts to 'well-paying job.' Michael is the assistant coach of Brandon's varsity baseball team. And Mason is the new head coach.

Oh dear god. How has this become my life?

Not knowing how to handle this, I step out onto the porch and close the front door, some innate voice telling me that inviting him inside would not be the appropriate thing to do. It could send mixed signals that I'm interested. I should be. I'd be crazy not to want to go out on another date with him.

"So, in the neighborhood, huh?" I ask, walking over to the new porch swing Brandon helped me put up last month. The distressed wood creaks when I sit down.

Michael's handsome face displays a playful wince. "Not really. Truth?"

I nod.

"I just wanted to see you. I had a great time last night. I thought, maybe, you'd like to do it again."

*Say yes, dummy.*

"I had a great time with you too."

Michael takes a seat next to me on the swing, his long legs splayed out in front of him. The green flecks in his pale brown eyes catch the light of the lowering sun.

"They're doing Shakespeare in the Park next weekend. *Romeo and Juliet.*"

I love outdoor theater. I don't care what's playing. Mason took me to see *The Lost Colony* in Manteo during fall break. We spent the week touring the Northern Outer Banks. Each day was filled with so much fun, and every night was filled with mind-blowing passion. After that trip was when I knew I was hopelessly, completely, and desperately in love with him. I started to dream big dreams and wish for a future that I had no idea would cease to exist as a possibility three months later.

Michael tips my chin up with a finger when I fail to answer.

And I hate that I feel... nothing. No zap of electricity or the chilling tingles of millions of goose bumps as they race along my skin. I don't feel that out-of-control need to have his hands and his lips touch every inch of me, take everything from me, like I did with Mason last night.

As much as I wish I was, I'm not attracted to Michael in that way. I don't feel anything toward him other than a burgeoning friendship. It wouldn't be right for me to string him along or lead him to think that I'm up for more than that.

"Michael, I don't—"

"There's another reason I came by."

Regaining my train of thought, I try to come up with a viable excuse to say no to the invitation for a second date I feel he's about to make. I don't want to hurt his feelings or make things awkward between him and Brandon since he's one of Brandon's coaches. I guess I should have thought about that before I agreed to go out with him. In my defense, I never expected my ex to show up again and tilt my world on its axis.

If things were different, I would somersault over myself for another date with Michael. It would give me more time to get to know him better. People who aren't attracted to each other at first can grow that attraction through conversation and things they have in common. Or so I've read.

But that was before.

It's funny how your entire life can change in the blink of an eye, or in my case, in less than twenty-four hours.

"I forgot to do something last night," he says, and leans in, taking me by surprise when he brushes his lips, ever so lightly, across mine.

This is wrong. It feels wrong.

Pulling back, I place a hand on Michael's chest to stop him from trying to kiss me again.

"Am I interrupting anything?"

*Oh no.*

*No no no.*

My stomach plummets when I see Mason standing at the bottom step of my porch, the look on his face telling me that, yes, he saw Michael kiss me.

Well, crap.

# CHAPTER 9

## *MASON*

I've been on my front porch watering the million plants Mama Mac had bought and dumped on me. She said she wanted me to have a pop of color. What I actually got was a recreation of the Amazon jungle and no garden hose since it's one of the many things I still need to purchase for the house. It also means that I've been going back and forth from the porch to the kitchen for the last half hour filling up glasses with tap water.

Just as I empty the last glass in the potted red hibiscus, a Ford Raptor pulls into Aria's driveway and a man gets out. And yeah, I may stand there and blatantly watch and listen to them, up until the point when he leans over and kisses her. That's when my feet decide to take authority over my brain and walk me across the yard to next door.

"Michael, I don't think—"

"Am I interrupting anything?"

I know I am by the way Aria goes stiff like the proverbial kid who gets caught with their hand in the cookie jar. Her head slowly swivels in my direction, and her pretty mouth drops open when she sees me standing there.

I'm known for having a quick temper. To punch first and ask questions later. That knee-jerk response is a direct result of the shitty childhood I was forced to endure, being thrown around like discarded refuse from one foster family to another my entire life. So, it's taking everything I have in me not to storm up the steps and punch this dickhead in the face for kissing my woman. Because make no mistake, Aria is mine, and she more than proved that last night by the way she kissed me like the world would end if she didn't.

"Mason, it's not what you—" Aria begins, then snaps her mouth shut when dickhead stands up and offers me his hand to shake.

"Hi, I'm Michael," he introduces himself.

I take his proffered hand and grip it, then notice the Dearborne High School baseball logo on the T-shirt he's wearing.

"Your last name wouldn't be Davies, would it?" I ask him.

I'm pretty sure the man whose hand I'm shaking, who just had his lips on Aria's, is the assistant coach I'm supposed to meet next. Great. I can't punch him now.

His momentary surprise eases into a polite smile. "Yeah. How'd you know?"

"I'm Mason McIntyre."

At the mention of my name, his eyes flare wide, and his handshake becomes overly enthusiastic.

"Holy shit! I didn't recognize you. It's so nice to meet you. I about freaked when they told me you were coming on board. I'm a huge fan. CU Wildcats all the way." Still shaking my hand with apparently no plans to let go anytime soon, he looks over at Aria. "*You* know Mason McIntyre?"

Her face goes up in flames when we lock eyes, and she catches my knowing smirk. The smirk that says I know her very, *very* well. Every inch of her. Carnally.

Michael goes on without waiting for her to reply, not stopping with his zealous handshake.

"Mason holds the collegiate record for fastest pitch at one hundred and seven point eight miles per hour, almost beating out Nolan Ryan's record of one-oh-eight point one. If he had been playing in the MLB, it would've ranked in the top five fastest pitches ever," he excitedly tells her.

It was one hundred and seven point nine miles per hour, actually, but whatever. And yes, Aria does know that tidbit of baseball fact because she was at the game and witnessed it firsthand.

As she and I continue to stare at one another, her face softens into a smile at the memory of that day.

When my arm gets tired, I give a casual tug, and Michael finally lets go.

"Why didn't you go into the majors? I'm surprised you didn't sign with the Lone Stars like your brother, Bennett."

I don't correct him about Bennett not being my brother because to Bennett and me, we are. He and Carter are my brothers in every true sense of the word. You don't have to share DNA to be a family.

And why didn't I go into the majors like Bennett did? I get asked that question a lot. The simple answer is, I didn't want to. I had a few teams interested in signing me, offers of multi-million-dollar contracts, and I walked away from all of it.

Some people said I was out of my mind for throwing it away. But baseball wasn't my passion. Never was. I only played to be with Bennett and Carter. To have an escape from my crappy life. I didn't know until much later that the McIntyres paid for everything so I could play. Uniforms. Bats. Balls. Gloves. Cleats. Helmets. I never questioned where it all came from. The only time I stopped playing was when I lived with that nicer foster family in Asheville for a couple of years. Without Bennett and Carter, I just didn't have the heart to play.

I don't realize that I've zoned out on what Michael is saying until I feel Aria's arm loop through mine.

"I'm so sorry. I didn't realize it was *that* time," she says, and I think she's talking to Michael until she pinches me on the underside of my arm.

I look down at her, and she bugs her eyes at me.

"What?" I silently mouth.

She pinches my arm again. "For dinner. I must have lost track of the time. Give me a sec to go change." She gives Michael an exuberant smile. "It was so nice of you to drop by. And thank you again for last night. With my work schedule and deadlines, it's been a while since I was able to go out with a *friend* and unwind."

She emphasizes the word *friend* and leans in closer to me, her grip on my arm tightening as her wide, fake smile remains plastered to her face.

My brain is slow to process, but when it does, understanding hits. This is the guy she went out on a date with last night. The guy I surreptitiously eavesdropped her mumbling about. The nice guy she wouldn't let kiss her.

Michael looks at her and at how she's clinging to me like a limpet. His forehead wrinkles with a slight frown.

"I didn't know you two were…"

Aria's imploring verdant eyes gradually narrow when a smile slowly begins to creep across my face. She just opened a metaphorical door for me, and I'm more than happy to waltz right on through. She wants me to play along as her boyfriend to get rid of him? I can absolutely do that.

"We used to date in college and recently reconnected." Which is the truth.

Aria nods her head emphatically. "Yes, that's right. It was very recent. So new in fact, we haven't told anyone yet."

"We were planning on telling Brandon tonight at dinner. Isn't that right, ladybug?"

She sucks in a surprised breath when I palm her pert ass and kiss the top of her head.

Aria smiles sweetly up at me, and I wince when she pinches me for a third time. Hard. I retaliate by pinching her ass cheek, and she jumps with a startled yelp, then scowls at me through her fake smile that's still cemented in place.

"I'm a lucky man. Not many guys get a second chance with the girl of their dreams."

Michael fidgets in place, looking uncomfortable as the silence between us lingers when no one says anything more. Eventually, he's the first to crack.

"I guess congratulations are in order. I'm really happy for the both of you." He peers behind him where his truck is parked like he's trying to figure out the best way to escape without being rude. "I should get going."

"It was nice to see you, Michael. Thank you again for a lovely dinner last night."

"Uh, yeah. You're welcome." His eyes briefly flit to me, sweat starting to bead along his forehead that has nothing to do with the early sweltering summer evening. "Nothing happened. I mean, nothing happened last night. I swear. Just friends, like she said," he hastily stammers.

I take pity on him.

"I know. We're good, man."

He blows out a relieved breath. "Okay, then."

Michael seems like a nice guy. If it were any other woman other than Aria, I'd feel sorry for the brush off she's giving him.

Since Aria is still clinging to me, I hold out a fist for him to bump to avoid another exuberant, long-winded handshake.

"I'll see you next Wednesday at the school meeting."

He taps my fist, then gives Aria a polite nod. "Yep. Looking forward to it. Have a good evening."

"You too," Aria replies and gives him a wave goodbye.

We watch from the porch as he gets into his truck and backs out of her driveway. As soon as he drives off, Aria removes her arm from mine and tries to slip away.

"I don't think so, sweetheart."

I grab her hips and back her up to the front door, caging her in with my body.

A hot breeze whips across the porch, bringing with it the teasing scent of wild honeysuckle.

"Mason, what are you doing?" she breathily asks, her cheeks flushing a pretty pink as she looks anywhere but directly at me.

"You started it," I inform her.

I shift closer until I can feel the pounding of her heart against my chest.

"You know full well I only said that to—"

She gasps, then bites her bottom lip with a moan when I lean in and caress my lips up the column of her neck only to find that the sweet honeysuckle fragrance is coming from her.

"So, dinner, huh?" I ask, taking the fleshy lobe of her ear and gently biting it.

"Mason, stop it," she weakly admonishes, then tilts her head to give me better access to explore, which I happily do.

I trace the shell of her ear with my lips and lightly blow, enjoying the way she shivers.

"What's for dinner?" I ask for her benefit because what

I'm hungry for is standing right in front of me.

"I already made dinner. I was going to drop it off."

"You made me dinner?"

"No. Yes. No. I mean, I made... pesto pasta... and..." Her voice hitches, and she grips the front of my shirt, bunching the fabric in her tight grasp. "I can't think straight when you do that."

My mouth curves on her skin. "Good."

"Mason, I'm serious... *Oh god*," she hums in pleasure when I brush a feathery kiss behind her ear where I remember she's most sensitive.

Her breathing becomes erratic until she's almost panting. I ghost my lips at her temple.

"You made pesto pasta?"

I kiss the side of her mouth, and she whimpers.

"Yes."

My fingertips follow the path of her curves as they glide up from her hips to her ribcage.

"For me?"

Her eyes flutter close when I trail a fingertip along her clavicle. Back and forth. A lazy seduction. Every muscle in her body is trembling with desire and need.

She swallows thickly. "Yes," she whispers.

Knowing that she made one of my favorite meals for me makes me stupidly happy.

"I bought a rotisserie chicken, too."

She rises on tiptoe, her lips chasing mine as I tease her face with phantom brushstrokes of my mouth. Her cheek, her forehead, her brow. When I don't give her what she wants, she growls at me.

"That's good because I'm starving." I reach around her and turn the doorknob to the front door.

"Me too," she says, twisting my shirt in her hands and

yanking me inside the house as soon as the door gives way.

# CHAPTER 10

## *ARIA*

My body is literally on fire. An inferno. I'm dry kindle ignited by the match of his teasing kisses. Singed. Branded.

Mason and I were combustible from the minute we met. We burned hot and wild. The chemistry between us was off the charts. For an inexperienced, naïve girl who had never been in a serious relationship before, being with Mason was new and exciting and life-altering. I became addicted to him. Craved him. Needed him. I never regretted a second of our time together. I only regretted... *still regret*... how we ended. The suddenness of it. The fact that I told him I loved him, and he couldn't say it back. Instead, he walked away, shattering my heart in the process and leaving a big, gaping crack splitting me wide open. A wound that had been slowly healing, only to be ripped apart again last night when he suddenly reappeared in my life. Declaring his intentions. Saying he came for me.

I'd be stupid to trust him with my heart again. It won't survive another Mason-sized crack when he inevitably walks away. I had decided earlier to give a tentative friendship between us a chance. Nothing more. He's my new neighbor, after all, and will be Brandon's coach once school starts. It's best we keep things casual and simple

—for my brother's sake, of course. He doesn't need any more drama in his life. Our parents' messy divorce and his strained relationship with his father are enough for a seventeen-year-old to handle.

Knowing all this, why am I dragging Mason inside my house ready to strip my clothes off and pounce him?

Because his lips on my skin feel good. Because it's been way too long since I've felt anything. Joy. Passion. Desire. And I want more. Damn the consequences.

And because, when it boils down to the ugly, messy truth, I'm still irrevocably in love with him.

We stumble over the threshold, mouths locked in a greedy, toe-curling kiss. It's desperate and uncoordinated— and probably one of the best kisses I've ever had.

Mason's capable hands lift me up, and my legs automatically lock around his lean waist as he carries me to who knows where. I don't care at this point as long as he doesn't stop kissing me.

I'm a little confused when he takes me into the kitchen and deposits me on top of the countertop, but that thought flies off into the ether when he steps between my thighs and kisses the hell out of me.

"Where're your plates, baby?"

"Huh?" my addled brain asks but sends the message to my arm on which cabinet to point to.

My fingers tug on the hem of his shirt, greedy to explore the hard plains of his torso.

"Forks?"

Since my hands are busy, my head indicates with an angled tilt which drawer to pull open.

*Finally*, I mentally cheer when his shirt is bunched up enough for me to seal my lips over his sun-kissed, tanned chest. His skin is warm and smooth like satin. As my lips attack his torso, my hands frenetically grapple the button and zipper of his shorts.

A long masculine finger eases my chin up until I'm forced to meet Mason's blue eyes. They scorch me with their desire as they slowly drag across my face, his intense visual inspection making my core throb with anticipation.

"Ready to eat?"

The deep huskiness of his voice causes tingling goose bumps to erupt from my neck to my ankles.

If by eat, he means hot, sweaty, mindless sex, then, yes.

Mason presses a kiss to my forehead, then to the tip of my nose. "Brandon, could you grab the pan with the pasta?"

My eyes flutter closed at the sweetness of his kisses, then immediately pop wide open.

Brandon?

The lust clouding my senses evaporates quicker than a raindrop on a hot sidewalk when my brother replies, "On it."

Oh. My. God.

How much did he see? When did he get here? How long has he been standing in the kitchen?

"Hope bottled water, soda, or iced tea is okay. That's about all we have," I hear Brandon say through the sheer panic and mortification quickly overtaking me.

"Ladybug, your choice. Water, soda, or iced tea?" Mason casually asks me, like my hand isn't currently shoved down his shorts and inside his underwear.

I blink. Blink again.

"Iced tea," I automatically answer, then... being about as subtle as an elephant in a room full of mice, I jerk back when I realize where my hand is. I'm going to hell.

The smirking grin he sends me just adds to my flustered state.

Spurred into action by absolute embarrassment, I slide off the counter and slip out from under Mason. I don't get far when he curls a finger in my belt loop and reels me back in. I push, and he pulls.

"*Mason.*"

"Aria."

Picking up the foil-covered glass baking pan, Brandon watches our tug-of-war with amused interest.

"Inside or outside?" he asks.

Two sets of male eyes look at me and wait for an answer.

I sigh in defeat, clearly outnumbered. "Outside."

"I'll grab the blanket." Brandon uses his foot to slide the back door open, then disappears out onto the deck.

After Mom and Dirk married, I started coming up with silly "traditions" to do with Brandon, like Sunday pancakes or Christmas Eve movie nights where we would pile blankets and pillows on the floor next to the tree and eat all the sugar cookies we made while watching *Die Hard*—which is totally a Christmas movie, no matter what anyone says. Another thing we liked to do was have picnic dinners under the stars, which we did often. Brandon and I have kept up our traditions over the years, and I'll miss them, miss him, when he goes off to college and starts adulting.

"He's a good kid. Has a much better head on his shoulders than I did at eighteen. You're doing a great job with him, Aria."

I hear the pride in his compliment, and something else... something that sounds like sadness.

"He's my brother. I love him," is my candid, truthful response.

I'd do anything for Brandon. Sacrifice anything. It's why I'm here in Dearborne. Brandon needed me.

"And he knows it. That's what's most important. He

knows he's loved and that your love is permanent. He can rely on it. Feel safe in it. Trust that it will always be there. Not everyone is so lucky."

The heaviness of what he says settles over me, cinching my heart. Even though he's referring to Brandon, he's also referring to himself. I think I'm starting to understand now. It's like a light bulb moment. A grand epiphany. Mason is scared to love. He's scared to have someone love him. That's why he couldn't say it to me that night. The concept of someone loving him terrifies him. He grew up transient, shuffled from one family to the next. Mason told me a little about his life. Not much, but enough for me to know there was so much more buried deep in the darkness. Bad things. He had no one who cared. No one permanent in his life who truly loved him. Not until Bennett and Carter. But the love of friendship and brotherhood is different from the love I wanted to give him. Tried to give him. He didn't trust it. Didn't trust it would last. Is that why he walked away?

*But he came back.*

Yeats wrote a poem, "Never Give All the Heart." It was one of Mason's favorites from my book that he would often read to me while we cuddled in bed. The poem spoke to men, advising them to never give their love to one woman because that love wouldn't last, and the man would be left heartbroken when the woman eventually walked away. I often wondered why he would go back to that one poem. In his own way, Mason opened up to me. Allowed me to see his vulnerability. I just didn't know it then.

With a hand, I reach up and cup the face of this beautifully tragic man. His head lists to one side, sinking into my touch. I take a step back when Brandon pokes his head inside.

"Hurry up. I'm starving. You guys can make out later."

"Brandon!"

Mason just laughs, picks up the rest of the stuff, and carries it outside with a "you coming?"

With those two simple innocuous words, my thoughts dive right down into the gutter.

# CHAPTER 11

## *ARIA*

Lying on the blanket, I peer up at the night sky as the warm summer's breeze fans its florally perfumed breath over my face. Our picnic dinner ended a little while ago. Brandon left to spend the night with his friend Nico, who lives in the cul-de-sac at the end of the street.

My body is snuggled to Mason's side, his arm cushioning the back of my head like a pillow, lulling me into a peaceful bliss I haven't felt in a long time. I gave up trying to figure out this *'whatever the heck it is'* between us hours ago and decided to just let what happens, happen—regardless of how that mindset completely goes against my Type C nature. I didn't even know there was a C personality until I took one of those career-slash-personality aptitude tests in high school. For someone like me who is cautious and logical, I'm starting to understand that sometimes in life, I don't have to have all the answers. Sometimes, it's okay to sit back and enjoy the journey without knowing the final destination.

"I found a unicorn."

Mason pulls me closer, and a swarm of excited butterflies flutters wildly inside my chest when his head leans in until we're cheek to cheek. I get distracted by the rasp of his day's growth of stubble and how his subtle cologne invades my lungs.

"Show me."

Straightening my arm, I reach up to trace the pattern for him, connecting the starry dots with my finger.

"It looks more like a banana with feet."

Giggles tumble out of me. "It does not. Look." I connect the stars again for him. "See, there's its body and there's the horn."

"Still a banana."

"Whatever. Clearly, you have no artistic vision."

"And you're just figuring that out now?" he teases.

Mason rolls onto his side, facing me, and those butterflies inside my chest explode into bombs of confetti when he tickles his index finger over the bridge of my nose. My breath catches as sparks of desire shoot straight between my thighs.

"What are you doing?"

Is that my voice, all wispy and needy?

"Creating my own constellation," he quietly replies, his face filled with concentration as he looks down at me.

Memories of long-ago rainy mornings come flooding back. Mason would spend hours drawing a finger over my skin from one freckle to the next as we laid in bed and listened to the music of the raindrops pattering against the windowpane.

I close my eyes and focus on the images he's drawing. A tiny heart on my nose. What feels like a flower with looping circles for petals on my cheek. His finger slowly glides down to my mouth, and my lips part as he languidly outlines their shape. I can feel the weight of his gaze on me as it follows the pattern his finger makes. I open my eyes when the kiss I want more than anything I've ever wanted in my life never comes.

"What are you thinking about?" I ask him after long seconds pass.

Even though he's gazing down at me, his eyes are unfocused and far away.

"Did I ever tell you about my mother? My biological one?"

A half dozen different emotions scurry through me including disbelief and hope.

Mason didn't talk much about his time in foster care. If I ever asked a direct question, he would shut the conversation down completely—so him opening up to me now is huge. All I can think is, *finally*. He's *finally* letting me in.

I shake my head no.

"I found her."

Mason carefully rolls over to lie on his back, then pulls me to his side until I'm half lying on top of him. I pillow my head on his chest and listen to the steady rhythm of his heartbeat.

"I had so many questions. So many things I wanted to ask. What was so wrong with me that she decided being my mom wasn't worth it? Who my father was and what happened to him. Did she ever love me? Was I a mistake? I needed to move forward, let the past and my anger go so I could be the man you deserved. To do that, I needed closure. Right after we came back from our trip to the Outer Banks, I started looking." He chuckles but it sounds off.

I lift my head and rest my chin on his chest. "You did?"

He never said anything to me about it.

He tucks a piece of my hair behind my ear. "Yeah."

I'm afraid to ask but do anyway. "What happened? Did you get to meet her?"

"No, baby, I didn't. She passed away sixteen years ago."

My lungs refuse to expand, his words splitting my heart in two and bleeding it dry. I cradle his face between my hands as I cry tears that I have no way of stopping.

"Mason, I am *so* sorry."

It's the only thing I can think to say. Because, honestly, what can you say to that?

He dries my wet cheeks with the pads of his thumbs.

"Finding out screwed me up mentally, and I went into a very dark place. I didn't want to drag you down with me. I couldn't let that darkness touch you."

"When did you find out?"

His eyes fix on mine. "The day before New Year's Eve."

And there it is. The answer to the question that has haunted me for the past year and a half: why he walked away and broke up with me.

My heart aches for this man. He's had to live through so much heartbreak, pain, and disappointment.

"Thank you for telling me."

His strong hands grip under my shoulders and slide me up his torso until I'm fully lying on top of him, our bodies aligned from head to toe, our mouths scant inches apart.

"I should have told you sooner, and I'm sorry I didn't. I'm sorry for so many things. But most of all, I'm sorry it took me so long to find my way back to you."

*Find my way back to you.* I absolutely melt into a puddle of emotional goo.

Trying to lighten things up, I reply, "Tampa isn't that far away."

"Tampa and therapy," he amends, but he's smiling when he says it.

It should sound like the punchline to a joke, but it's not.

I want to ask him about both, but don't because his mouth meets mine, his kiss reverent and sweet.

"You once told me that you loved me."

At the reminder of that night, it feels like a fist shoves its way through my chest.

"Mason, I don't want to talk about—"

His lips stop my protest with another kiss.

"Let me finish."

"Mason, I—"

Another kiss.

Lust and irritation commingle. "Stop kissing me to—"

He kisses me again, this time deeper and longer until every thought flies right out of my head.

"You told me that night that you loved me." He grips my face between his hands, his blue eyes firing like sapphire embers in the dark. And then my entire world explodes apart when he says, "But what I never told you was... I love you too, Aria. So damn much."

I forget how to breathe.

My lungs literally forget how to function.

He said them. The words.

I can't believe he just said them.

*I love you.*

Three words that completely destroy me in the best way possible.

Mason *loves* me.

A waterfall of tears cascades down my cheeks, unbidden, and I can't stop them.

"What?" I choke out, not believing what I heard.

Mason sits us up and holds me close, his own tears joining mine.

"I love you."

*Oh god.*

I sob uncontrollably as what he said loops round and round in a dizzying swirl.

*He loves me.*

"Baby, please don't cry. I'm so sorry for hurting you. If you can find a way to forgive me—" Mason reaches between us and places his open hand over my pounding, overjoyed heart. "—I swear on my life, I will protect this, cherish and love it, until my dying breath."

Do I trust it? More importantly, can I trust *him*? I search my soul for the answers as I stare into his ocean blue eyes. It's in those endless pools of deep blue that I find the truth.

"Say it again."

His gorgeous face breaks out with the most beautiful smile I've ever seen. "I love you."

"Mason?"

"Yeah, baby?"

Steeling my courage, I lean back in his arms and bluntly state, "Take me to bed."

His pupils dilate until the blue is completely eclipsed. An excited tremor skims up my body at what that heated midnight gaze entails. And I want it. Badly. I don't want soft or sweet or tender. There'll be time for all that later.

His voice is gruff when he asks, "Are you sure?"

With a sole-minded determination, I grip his hair at the back of his head and nip his bottom lip, making it clear what I want.

Rough hands dig into the flesh of my ass to secure me in place as he rises to stand while holding me in his arms. A physical feat that should be impossible, but one he makes look ridiculously easy. And hot as hell.

Locking my ankles at the curve of his lower lumbar, he adjusts his grip to palm my ass with one hand while the other presses on my lower back. The hard length of him strokes my clit through our clothes, and I moan. Loudly. I know as soon as he touches me down there—with his mouth, fingers, or, *yes, please,* the massive hardness I'm trying my best to grind down on—I'm going to go off like the fourth of July.

I haven't had sex since the last time he and I were together. Pitiful, I know, but Mason ruined me for anyone else. Completely, thoroughly, devastatingly ruined me.

Because no matter how much I wanted to move on this past year, I couldn't. Just like I couldn't stop loving him.

"Baby," he begins, but this time, it's me shutting him up with a hard kiss.

"If you ask me again if I'm sure, I'm going to strangle you. Now kindly take me inside and screw my brains out."

There. Straight to the point. No mincing words.

His grin turns wicked, one filled with delicious promises.

I think I just had a mini orgasm.

# CHAPTER 12

## *MASON*

With our kiss out of control and my hands full of her soft curves, I stumble inside Aria's house with her locked tightly around me.

"Brandon," I grunt against her mouth.

"Won't be home until tomorrow," she pants out.

Thank god.

I push her up against the wall on our way to her bedroom, not able to wait any longer to feel her skin under my fingertips.

"Here's good." She goes for the zipper of my shorts. "Off."

Not needing any further convincing, as long as I'm inside her in the next five seconds, I tug the back of her shirt, but it gets stuck between my hand, her back, and the wall.

"You first."

Forget this. I have plans for my beautiful Aria. I've been without her for far too long. Hundreds of days to make up for. So many orgasms I owe her.

"Mason," she whines when I turn us and begin walking again.

"Patience, ladybug. Which one?" I ask, and she absentmindedly points to the bedroom door to the left as her mouth does delicious things to my neck.

The door is cracked open, so I push it with my foot, then kick it closed once we cross the threshold. There'll be time later to look around her personal space and be nosy, but my sole focus is getting her in bed and naked, in that order.

Laughter explodes out of her when I tumble us to the mattress, the soft goose-down comforter cushioning our descent.

Her laughter suddenly dies, and the smile creasing her cheeks gradually diminishes as we lock eyes, the air surrounding us electrifying, pulsing like a physical thing. Like lightning in a bottle.

This moment right here... this incredible thing between Aria and me... this boundless love between us that refused to die and only grew stronger even though distance and time separated us... is *everything*.

With reverence, I gaze down at her, memorizing every detail, every new freckle, every minute change, getting lost in the gold halo surrounding the verdant green of her eyes.

"You are so goddamn beautiful."

Her eyes turn into emerald pools as unshed tears gather.

"I've missed you. So much." She lifts a delicate hand to my face and brushes the pad of her thumb across my bottom lip, licking her lips as she does, like she's savoring the taste of our last kiss.

My cock, which has been aching and hard for her most of the evening, wants to feel those soft lips wrapped around it. Not tonight, but soon. Tonight, I want to make love to my woman.

With a gentleness that belays the fierce desire consuming me, I softly kiss her. But Aria has other plans.

She pushes on my chest until I rise to my knees. Her intense perusal travels over me, scorching me to cinder and ash. My heart rate triple beats when her gaze fixates on the bulge trapped behind my board shorts, trying to bust free, eager to be deep inside her.

"Baby, stop looking at me like that," I warn her.

"Like what?" she asks a little breathlessly, eyes going wide, then, "You look..." She scrapes her bottom lip between her teeth and peers up at me. "*Bigger.*"

A huge smile spreads across my face. No better ego boost. "Yeah?"

She playfully rolls her eyes. "Get over yourself."

I'm laughing as I tackle her back onto the bed and kiss her stupid.

Happiness.

I realize that's the emotion bursting through me as I kiss Aria over and over. It's a feeling I haven't been acquainted with in a long time. Not since I walked away from her. Men like me don't get many second chances, and I will not screw up this miracle again. She's it for me. The one person who owns me completely—heart, body, and soul.

Something Jordan, Douglass's husband, once told me pops into my mind. It's something his mother told him. "*One day, this incredible person will walk into your life and flip it upside down in the most amazing way possible. You'll finally understand the meaning and the gravitas of the words 'I love you;' not because you say them, but because they are embedded into your soul and tattooed onto your heart. It's then you realize you found your soulmate.*"

"I love you."

I can't seem to stop saying it now, and Aria deserves a lifetime of hearing it.

With me still kneeling in front of her on the bed, she pulls her T-shirt over her head and tosses it who knows where, then does the same to mine. In a similar gesture to the one I did, Aria takes my hand and presses my palm flat to her chest right above where her heart beats strong.

"This belongs to you. It's always been yours, Mason. And if you don't make love to me right this second—"

God, I love this woman.

I crush my mouth to hers, and she immediately opens, allowing me inside to taste her. To savor her. Our bodies move in a sybaritic dance as the rest of our clothes are shed, piece by piece. Claiming every inch of her soft skin, I lick and kiss a path across her chest, her breasts, her stomach, the curve of her hip, listening as her sighs turn to moans the farther down her body I go. I brush my nose across her trimmed pubis, inhaling her scent, drowning in it.

No teasing. No preamble. No build up. I just feast.

Her back arches off the bed, and she cries out when I go straight for her clit. Adding one finger, then another, I slide them along her inner wall, locating her G-spot with ease. It takes less than a minute before her delirious moans turn into screams of my name as her orgasm slams into her. And I watch every second of it. How her back curves, head thrown back, eyes closed, and dark hair spilling over the pillow. Absolutely breathtaking.

"*Mason*. Holy shit. That was…"

Her grip on my hair tightens, and she uses it to pull me up her body. She moans again when I kiss her, and she tastes herself on my lips.

"Now," she demands, wrapping her legs around me and planting her bare feet to the backs of my thighs so she can push me forward, begging me with her body to fill her. My cock aches for it. Wants it more than my lungs need air to breathe.

But I'm a greedy man and not done with her yet. Remembering how sensitive her breasts are, I spend long minutes kissing and caressing each one until she's writhing under me.

"Mason, *please*."

I take a nipple into my mouth and lightly bite down, enjoying how her entire body shudders.

"Please what?"

She reaches between us and circles her hand around my aching cock, and I almost come right then.

"Please stop teasing me," she says as her hand begins to slowly move, stroking me until I'm the one panting.

Her smile is pure sin. I'm not the only tease. I also can't hold back any longer.

"Do we need to have the condom talk?" she asks, not stopping the rhythm of her hand as it pumps up and down my length.

Her question sounds casual, but it's far from it. She wants to know if I've been with anyone else. The answer is a solid hell no.

"I haven't been with anyone since you."

I hadn't noticed how tense she'd been while waiting for my reply until now.

"Me either."

Good to know. It wouldn't have mattered. Made me insanely, murderously jealous? Absolutely. But the past is just that—the past, exactly where it belongs. No more looking back. No more letting it control me. The only thing that matters is the woman under me. Our present and our future.

With one smooth thrust, I enter her. Aria mewls out her pleasure, moans my name. I'm making it my mission to hear those sounds over and over all night long.

Not breaking our connection, I gather her in my arms and lift her up. She wraps every part of herself around me as I hold her close, chest to chest. And we begin to move.

Our lips meet, our kiss slow and sensuous, mimicking the languid tempo of our lovemaking. One hand drops to her hip to help steady her as she rides me. The roll of her hips is torture of the best kind. When her inner walls begin to flutter, telling me she's close, I ease her back to lie on the bed and lift her left leg by bend of her knee, opening her more fully for my next thrust.

Slow turns into punishing. Languorous into feverish.

Aria breaks our kiss and buries her face in my neck as I pound into her, taking her higher and higher. Giving everything I have to go deeper. Harder. Telling her with my body how much I love her. That she's mine. But words are nice, too.

"Aria, I have loved you since the day we met," I tell her, pulling out then pushing back in. Wet, warm. Perfect. "I loved you before, I love you now. I will love you always."

"Don't you dare make me cry right now."

Too late. I see the lovely, lone tear escape, and I kiss it away.

I drive into her over and over again, pushing her for more. I angle in and hit the spot deep inside of her that I know will cause her to detonate within seconds.

Just as her walls clamp down, Aria cries out, chanting that she loves me too. She bows in my arms, and I bury my face between her breasts as the force of her orgasm obliterates every nerve ending in my body and triggers my own release.

She goes boneless as I collapse on top of her. We're slicked with sweat and utterly spent. Remembering how much she enjoys feeling my body weight pressing her down, I cage her in and brush butterfly kisses over her face as her shudders die down.

Her eyes are bright and her smile goofy. I'm sure my face wears a matching expression.

Touching a finger to the curve of her mouth, I ask, "Happy?"

"More than happy."

We grin at each other.

"Want to take a shower?"

"Depends."

She swipes a piece of my hair off my forehead. I return the favor by twirling a strand of her coal-black hair around my index finger and enjoy how the silken tress glides over my knuckle as it unfurls.

"On what?" I ask.

She takes me by surprise when she flips us over and straddles me. My cock immediately thickens.

Her mouth curves in wonder. "That was quick."

My ego does another fist pump in celebration.

Before I can respond with something witty—okay, more than likely something dirty—she says, "We'll get to the shower in a minute. But first…"

I don't have to wait to find out because Aria slithers down my body and sends me to heaven.

# CHAPTER 13

## *ARIA*

Lizzo's "Good as Hell" starts playing. Cuts off and starts again. Kama's ring tone.

With bright sunlight streaming in through the crack in the curtain, I slowly rouse and stretch, feeling sore in all the best places. Mason and I certainly made up for lost time last night. And this morning. The bed, the shower, the bed again, on the kitchen table when we went to grab a snack to eat at four in the morning, the wall in the hallway. And to make the entire night even more perfect, I fell asleep with my head on his lap as he read me Yeats from the book of poetry I keep on my nightstand.

Mason's sleep-husky, deep voice groans near my ear. "Your phone has been going off for the last five minutes."

"It's just Kama being nosy."

He chuckles. "Sounds like her."

Kama has always been Team Mason. She's going to flip when she hears that we're back together.

Mason smooths a hand up my leg, making me squirm. We're facing one another, our heads sharing the same pillow.

"Want me to get it?" he asks when it goes off again.

In answer, I snuggle back down into his warmth. I'm not

ready to move yet. Mason palms my ass and pulls me closer to him, kissing the side of my breast. Desire begins to swirl through me, but I tamp it down and enjoy my quiet cuddle time. I'm too sore anyway and will need a day or two to recover.

"What time is it?"

His lips touch my forehead. "Eight."

Which means I've only gotten about two hours of somewhat slumber. Brandon won't be back until this afternoon, so... I think a nap is in order.

Before sleep can reclaim me again, a delicious aroma tickles my nose and engages my brain. I squint one eye open and am met with Mason's blue-eyed, gorgeous face.

"Please tell me that's coffee and not me hallucinating."

"You're not hallucinating. There are also eggs, bacon, freshly squeezed orange juice, and triangles of toast, lightly buttered."

My heart goes all gooey and melty. He made me breakfast in bed.

"You made me breakfast?"

Just thinking about food has my stomach gurgling its hunger and making obscene noises.

With a long-fingered masculine hand, he wraps it around my throat and tips my chin up with his thumb so he can kiss me.

"I did."

"When?"

I didn't notice him get out of bed. Then again, four orgasms will make any woman comatose.

"Not too long ago. Maybe a half hour, tops. You have a lot of food in your kitchen."

"Have to feed a teenager. Their stomachs are bottomless pits. I bet you and Bennett ate Mama Mac out of house and home."

Which is a weird figure of speech because your house *is* your home. It's redundant.

"I plead the fifth."

"How is she doing?" I inquire.

I met Mama Mac a couple of times. Wonderful woman. Loving, open, and with the biggest heart of anyone I've ever met. She loves Mason like she loves her son, Bennett. It never mattered to her that Mason wasn't her biological child. He was hers. End of story.

"She's good and can't wait to see you. When you're up for it, she wants you over for Sunday supper."

At the mention of food again, my tummy flips.

"Absolutely. Tell her thank you."

"You can tell her yourself. She's coming over later with more plants." He groans. "Apparently, and I quote, 'You need more red.'"

So that's why Mason's front porch looks like a rainbow threw up on it.

He reaches over and lifts a steaming mug of coffee from a tray on the nightstand. I sit up, not caring that the sheet falls to my lap, leaving my naked chest on full display. Mason's eyes instantly focus on them and heat.

"Eyes up here, Romeo. Your woman needs an IV of black coffee, stat, food, and possibly an ice pack."

I take the coffee from him, pucker my lips and blow, which only makes his gaze burn hotter. I thought I was too sore, but the wetness between my thighs calls me a liar.

He holds some toast up to my mouth, and I take a bite.

"After breakfast, I want to do something."

He offers me a ripe, red strawberry, which I bite in half. Mason leans in and kisses the sweet juices from my lips.

"Mason, you know I suck at surprises."

"It's not really a surprise."

My interest piques. "Then what is it?"

"We'll do it after breakfast."

Bunching the bed sheet around me and cinching it together to hold it in place, I slip off the bed. My bare toes sink into the thick area rug. I love this rug. Brandon says it looks like I skinned the Abominable Snowman.

"Let's do it now."

He's already dressed in the shorts he wore yesterday, but he's not wearing a shirt. I become transfixed on all the muscles on display. His dark blond happy trail. That sexy V that frames his abs.

"Eyes up here, ladybug."

Enjoying way too much at being able to throw my words back at me, he smirks when I blush.

Mason locates his shoes on the floor at the foot of the bed and puts them on.

"Give me half a minute. I need to go get something from the house."

Alright, my interest is most definitely piqued now.

I follow him down the hallway and through the kitchen. He gives me a quick kiss, then disappears out the back patio door. Just like he promised, he's back in less than a minute.

I make a very unladylike squeal when he heads straight for me and lifts me in his arms, bridal style.

"Mason, put me down."

My protest is weak, as evidenced by the way my arms loop around his neck, because what woman in her right mind doesn't want to be carried like this by her man.

When he takes me out onto the deck, I exclaim, "Mason, I'm not dressed!"

"It'll take just a second."

The early morning sun is blinding, and I have to shade

my eyes with a hand.

"What if the neighbors see?"

"I'm your neighbor. And you're decent."

"I am not! I'm wearing a sheet."

My words fall on deaf ears as he pads down the steps and rounds the corner between our houses and stops in front of the Southern red oak.

"You kidnapped me to come outside with no clothes on for a tree?"

"Nope. I wanted to give you this."

He gently lowers me to my feet onto the dewed grass. I grip the sheet tightly to my chest for obvious reasons.

"Know what this tree reminds me of?" he asks.

I love how he sees it the same way I do.

"The Wishing Tree."

"Yep."

He takes something out of his pocket and places it in my hand.

It's a piece of wrinkled pink construction paper in the shape of a heart with a small hole at the top. The paper's edges are frayed, and the pink color bleached white in a few places.

At first, I'm confused. And then I see it. The cursive writing. It's barely legible, but I see it. Recognition slams into me.

"How?"

I can't even get the rest of the words out because I start bawling like a baby.

*I want Mason to love me.*

It's my wish. The one I wrote a dozen times and hung on the Wishing Tree at CU. How is it possible he has it?

He hands me another paper heart. This one new, the paper crisp and bright with a thin satin ribbon looped through the hole.

*Mason loves Aria.*

"I love you, Aria. You will never doubt it because I am going to fill the branches of this tree every day with paper hearts."

Our very own Wishing Tree.

Speechless, I look at him through tear-streaked eyes, my heart about to burst with the love I feel for him.

And by some miracle, or whatever magic exists in the world that grants wishes, he loves me back.

# EPILOGUE

## *FOUR MONTHS LATER*

## *ARIA*

*"Three... two... one. Happy New Year!"*

Standing next to the Wishing Tree, shivers dance along my spine as the chilly wind perforates through the thin wool of my peacoat. I flip the collar up and adjust my scarf as the wind whips the tiny snow flurries around and around like dancing wood sprites.

Only this time...

"Aria?"

His breath skates across my cheek, the way he says my name is a husky seduction that makes me weak in the knees.

"Yeah?" I ask, leaning back into him to enjoy the fireworks exploding above our heads.

Shimmering golden sparkles rain down all around us before more fireworks streak up into the cloud-covered sky. Each boom reverberates through my chest like cannon fire, matching the drum beat of my heart that only beats for Mason McIntyre.

"I love you."

*God.*

*God, this man.*

Warmth spreads through me like liquid fire that has nothing to do with the way his body is pressed against my backside. I tip my head back until it's resting on his shoulder. I can see the fireworks above reflect like a kaleidoscope in his denim blue eyes.

"I love you three thousand," I say back.

And yes, I know it's nerdy and comes from *Avengers: Endgame*, but whatever.

Mason kisses the tip of my nose. "I love it when you talk 'nerty' to me."

Nerdy plus dirty equals 'nerty.' It's our thing.

To say this has been the best New Year's would be an understatement. Mason surprised me with a trip back to CU to watch the fireworks. He said he wanted a New Year's do-over. A second chance. We've been here for a few days already, replacing old memories with new ones. Making *better* ones.

"Can I ask you a question?"

Without taking my eyes off the light show, I reply, "Sure."

He circles a strong arm around my bundled body, turning me in a half circle until—

*Oh my god.*

My gloved hand flies to my mouth when he drops to one knee, his hand reaching into his coat pocket and pulling out a small powder blue box.

A Tiffany box. Every woman knows exactly what that box entails while your man is on bended knee.

"Mason."

"Aria, you are my—"

I don't need him to verbalize the question. I don't need a flowery speech or sweet poetic verbiage. I don't need him to say anything at all. Because my answer will always be—

"Yes!" I shout.

His handsome face breaks out with a smile full of effervescent happiness.

"I haven't even asked you yet."

I fling myself on top of him, tackling him to the ground, much to the amusement of everyone around us. With all the layering and cold weather gear we're wearing, it's like trying to hug and kiss a marshmallow.

"I don't care. The answer is still yes!"

Snow speckles his forehead and rosy cheeks. His eyes bright with love. His dimpled smile wide and carefree. I love this wonderfully complicated man with all my heart.

"A million times yes," I say, tears of pure joy wetting the loose strands of my hair that are plastered to my face by my knit hat. "I love you, Mason McIntyre."

Mason kisses me with an unrestrained passion that could melt the falling snow, while simultaneously pulling the glove off my left hand and sliding the gorgeous diamond solitaire onto it.

"And I love you, soon-to-be Mrs. Aria McIntyre. Always and forever."

No sweeter words have ever been spoken.

## THE END

You can meet Mason for the first time in Wanderlost, my award-winning small-town romance. Mason also returns in About That Night. All my books are on Amazon and free to read with Kindle Unlimited.

Want a free novella? You can read Tate (A Fallen Brook short novella) for free just by signing up to my newsletter.

# ALSO BY THE AUTHOR

**Under Jennilynn Wyer (New Adult & College, Contemporary romance)**

**The Fallen Brook Series**

#1 All Our Next Times

#2 Paper Stars Rewritten

#3 Broken Butterfly

The Fallen Brook Boxed Set with bonus novella, Fallen Brook Forever

# 4 Reflections of You (Coming 2024)

**The Montgomerys: Fallen Brook Stand-alone Novels**

That Girl* [Aurora + JD]
* *Winner of the Rudy Award for Romantic Suspense*
* *A Contemporary Romance Writers Stiletto Finalist*

Wanderlost [Harper + Bennett]
* *Contemporary Romance Writers Reader's Choice Award Winner*
* *Contemporary Romance Writers Stiletto Finalist*
* *HOLT Medallion Finalist*
* *Carolyn Reader's Choice Award Finalist*

About That Night [Jordan + Douglass]

The Fallen Brook Romance Series: The Montgomerys box set

Love Everlasting [Mason + Aria's novella]

## Savage Kingdom Series: A dark, enemies to lovers, mafia, why choose romance

#1 Savage Princess
* *HOLT Medallion Finalist*

#2 Savage Kings

#3 Savage Kingdom

The Savage Kingdom Series is now available as audiobooks (Narrated by Keira Grace)

## Forever M/M Romance Series (A Fallen Brook Spin-off)

#1 Forever His (Julien's POV)
* *A Contemporary Romance Writers Stiletto Finalist*

#2 Forever Yours (Elijah's POV)

#3 Forever Mine (Dual POV)

## Beautiful Sin Series: A dark, enemies to lovers, reverse harem/why choose

#1 Beautiful Sin

#2 Beautiful Sinners

#3 Beautiful Chaos

**Under J.L. Wyer (High School & Young Adult)**

**The Fallen Brook High School Young Adult Romance Series: a reimagining of the adult Fallen Brook Series for a YA audience**

#1 Jayson

#2 Ryder

#3 Fallon

#4 Elizabeth

The Fallen Brook High School YA Romance Series Boxed Set (Books 1-4) with bonus alternate endings

**YA Standalones**

The Boyfriend List
*\* HOLT Medallion Award Winner*
*\* A Contemporary Romance Writers 2022 Stiletto Finalist*

# ABOUT THE AUTHOR

Jennilynn Wyer is multi-award-winning romance author (Rudy Award winner for Romantic Suspense, HOLT Medallion Award winner, Contemporary Romance Writers Reader's Choice Award winner, four-time Contemporary Romance Writers Stiletto Finalist, three-time HOLT Medallion Award Finalist, and a Carolyn Reader's Choice Award Finalist). She writes steamy, contemporary and New Adult romances as well as dark rh/why choose romances. She also pens YA romance under the pen name JL Wyer. Jennilynn is a sassy Southern belle who lives a real-life friends-to-lovers trope with her blue-eyed British husband. When not writing, she's nestled in her favorite reading spot, e-reader in one hand and a cup of coffee in the other, enjoying the latest romance novel.

### Connect with the Author

**Website:** https://www.jennilynnwyer.com
**Linktree:** https://linktr.ee/jennilynnwyer
**Email:** jennilynnwyerauthor@gmail.com
**Facebook:** https://www.facebook.com/ JennilynnWyerAuthor

**Twitter:** https://www.twitter.com/JennilynnWyer

**Instagram:** https://www.instagram.com/jennilynnwyer

**TikTok:** https://www.tiktok.com/@jennilynnwyer

**Goodreads:** https://www.goodreads.com/author/show/20502667.Jennilynn_Wyer

**BookBub:** https://www.bookbub.com/authors/jennilynn-wyer

**Books2Read:** https://books2read.com/ap/nAAgBb/Jennilynn-Wyer

**Amazon Author Page:** https://www.amazon.com/author/jennilynnwyer

**Newsletter:** https://forms.gle/vYX64JHJVBX7iQvy8

**SUBSCRIBE TO MY NEWSLETTER** for news on upcoming releases, cover reveals, sneak peeks, author giveaways, and other fun stuff!

### JOIN THE J-CREW: A JENNILYNN WYER ROMANCE READER GROUP

Join link https://www.facebook.com/groups/jennilynnsjcrewreadergroup